THE
SECRET
OF THE
SPHINX

SAMUEL BAVLI

Tambora Books

Cover design by Derek Murphy
Cover art by Evolvana (Sabrina Gris)

CONTENTS

CHAPTER 1

THE VIZIER

Neb was asleep when the door burst open and three armed men entered his chamber. Startled, Neb almost cried out, but he caught himself just in time. He was the king's vizier, the second most powerful man in all of Egypt, and it would not be proper for him to show fear.

"What is the meaning of this?" Neb demanded, sitting up in bed. "How dare you enter my room without permission!"

Two of the intruders positioned themselves at the door, their swords drawn, while their leader advanced a step towards Neb. The leader drew his sword from the scabbard at his side and waved the sword in the direction of Neb's clothing. "Get dressed," he ordered. "You are summoned."

"Who summons the king's vizier?" Neb asked.

"Just do as you are told. You'll find out when you get there," the leader answered gruffly.

Neb rose majestically and got dressed, keeping his anger to himself. Considering Neb's high position, only the king himself had the right to summon him in this way. But Neb did not think the summons had come from the king. Even if Neb had committed some terrible offense, he doubted that the king would have sent for him in so discourteous a manner. As angry as King Djedef-Ra might be, he still would have treated his vizier with the honor that Neb's title of *Tjaty* deserved. At the very least, the king would have respected Neb's magic powers.

In fact, Neb strongly suspected he was about to face one of his enemies. But which one? Surely a man in his position had many enemies. It was clear that his captors would give him no further information, so Neb decided it was best to play along with them for now. Soon enough, he would find out who had summoned him. And then, he would have to trust in his magic powers to save him from his enemy's grip.

Neb put on his loincloth. He snapped his golden collar of office around his neck, and on his finger he slipped the signet ring with the great seal of the king's vizier. After a moment's consideration, he covered himself with a long white robe to guard against the desert wind. When he had finished putting on his garments, he slipped on his sandals and strode towards the broken door.

The leader still held his unsheathed sword. "Hurry up, *Tjaty!*" he said, his tone of voice mocking Neb's official title, while the two underlings seized Neb by his arms and forcefully led him outside.

Neb shook himself awake and squinted in the dim torchlight. His joints ached from the long ride in an oxcart, during which he had been blindfolded, bound hand and foot, and drugged. He was not sure just how far away his captors had taken him, or even how much time the trip had taken. He thought he remembered being asleep for at least part of the trip, although he wasn't even sure of that. One thing he did know: he was no longer in the city, but somewhere in the vast Egyptian desert, in a secret, underground vault. He was no longer blindfolded, but his wrists were bound to a post. He was utterly alone.

In the distance, Neb saw torches mounted on the walls, but there were no torches near where he was sitting. He could just make out the writing on the walls and the brightly painted scenes of gods and goddesses. On the wall to his left, the jackal-headed god Anubis, who judged the souls of the dead, stood next to a large pair of scales. The writing below Anubis was a passage from the Book of the Dead.

At a short distance beyond Anubis, the god Osiris, the "dying god," king of the Underworld, was depicted with the tall white crown of Upper Egypt on his head; he was flanked by the goddess Isis and by the falcon-headed sky-god Horus.

But the most impressive painting was on the wall to Neb's right. There, an array of demons and beasts crouched beneath the huge figure of Set, god of disorder, deserts, storms, and war. Set, who had killed his own brother Osiris, stood in profile, holding the rod of power in his right hand. And Set's eye, placed just above his beak-like, pointed animal snout, glared wickedly at Osiris on the opposite wall.

Suddenly, Neb was aware of movement at the other end of the hall. Three forms stood in the flickering torch-light, partially hidden by thick smoke that curled upwards from the stone floor. For a long time they stood close together, apparently talking to each other, but Neb could not hear their voices.

Finally, the three figures separated and stood side by side. Slowly they advanced towards Neb.

Still hidden in the thick smoke, the middle figure spoke. "It is so good to see you here, Neb." The mocking voice echoed through the large hall. "Neb, the great vizier, keeper of the king's seal, overseer of the king's works, administrator of the Two Lands. And, of course, let us not forget, king's sorcerer. Where is your magic now, *Tjaty?*"

The smoke began to clear a little, and gradually the faces of Neb's enemies became visible. All three had animal heads like those of the gods painted on the walls. But the one who most attracted Neb's attention was the middle one, the one who had just now spoken, the one who was the leader of the three, the one responsible for Neb's capture: Neb's enemy. Neb turned his eyes from his enemy's face and glanced at the wall to his left. A shudder went up his spine. His vision was still somewhat blurred from the lingering effects of the drug he had been given on his way here, and he found it difficult to bring the faces completely into focus. But, as he turned his eyes forward again, there was no question that his enemy's face was the same as that of the jackal-headed god on the painted wall: it was Anubis, judge of the dead.

Neb was quite certain it was not really the great god standing before him, but only a man in a jackal-headed mask. Nevertheless, the effect on Neb was almost as great as if Anubis himself had indeed been standing there before him. Neb broke out in a cold sweat. Strange odors filled the air. His head felt light; his skin tingled. He felt as though the walls were closing in on him, and he imagined his jackal-headed enemy standing over him, gloating, as he slowly pressed his hand to Neb's throat, strangling him. Terrifying visions of monsters danced before Neb's eyes, and he was no longer certain whether the visions were imagined or real. The monsters growled and snapped at him as he sat helplessly bound to the post. He attempted to summon his magic but found he could not do so. He supposed it was the effect of the drug his captors had given him, blocking his magic powers. Or perhaps it was the effect of some new drug carried with the odors that filled the air.

Jackal-head moved closer to Neb. He raised his right hand, in which he held a pair of scales. "Hear this judgement," he said. "Your heart has been weighed in the Great Balance. Your soul has stood as a witness, and you have been found to be unworthy. Wickedness has been found in your heart, and you have done great harm. For this you will be punished."

"Do not speak to me about wickedness," said Neb. "It is you who are the evil one. Even from where I sit, I can feel the evil in your heart, and I know for sure that you are not the great god Anubis. You are, like me, a mortal man. And the 'punishment' of which you speak is merely your revenge on me, your enemy. But what have I done to you, and who are you? Why do you seek revenge?"

Jackal-head did not answer immediately. Neb waited as he watched his enemy. Again he tried to summon his magic powers, to see the face behind the jackal mask. However, even though Neb's head was clearer now, he was still unable to use even the slightest shred of magic.

Neb's mind was racing, trying to figure out why he couldn't use his powers. Suddenly Neb felt something in the air, like an invisible net surrounding him, binding him. It was only the slightest feeling, and only someone familiar with the magic arts could have detected it, but it was surely there, and Neb knew exactly what it was: the magic of another sorcerer, a sorcerer very nearby. His jackal-headed enemy.

"I see your far-famed magic is not so powerful after all," said jackal-head. "Perhaps, my lord vizier, you have finally met your match."

Neb did not answer but continued looking at his captor, trying to understand his purpose. Could it be that jackal-head was not seeking revenge at all but was just an upstart sorcerer testing his powers against the famous Neb? Neb quickly dismissed that idea. Even without his magic powers, Neb could sense the hatred in his captor's voice and feel the venom in his words.

Jackal-head moved around Neb, like an animal circling its prey. "Are you afraid?" he asked.

Neb continued looking at his enemy, silently.

"You *should* be afraid, you know. Most people would be, in your situation."

Neb's face showed no emotion, and his gaze remained firm. There was no visible sign of the fear that Neb felt in his heart. "You seem to have learned some magic," he said. "You have even succeeded in trapping me in your net. But you will not be able to kill me. Your power is not great enough for that."

"Oh no, *Tjaty*, I do not mean to kill you. You mistake my meaning, and you have hurt me greatly by even thinking I would want to kill you. But I will no longer tolerate your interference with my plans. I want you out of the way. And so, I have arranged for you to leave, never to return."

"Please excuse my ignorance," said Neb. "What plan of yours have I upset? I do not even know who you are."

"I am surprised at you, my lord vizier," said jackal-head. "I thought by now you would have figured out who I am. In all of Egypt, only you realized that the recent deaths of the king's two eldest sons were not accidental as they appeared to be. Even the king himself was convinced that their deaths were accidental. But you continued to suspect; even after many weeks of fruitless searching, you continued your investigation. Unfortunately, you were getting too close. It was just a matter of time before you would discover the proof you needed — before you would discover who killed the royal princes. Those deaths were my doing. But I am not yet finished. The king still has one son left alive, and I must also plan that son's untimely death."

Hatred and anger burned in Neb's eyes. "The king is a god. He is falcon-headed Horus here on earth in human form. How dare you plan to kill his son, his heir?"

"Ah, Neb," said jackal-head. "I am surprised at you. Surely you should know better. The king himself may be a god, but is his son a god? If he is a god, then Horus will protect him, and my attempt will fail. And if I do succeed in killing him, then it is clear he is no god at all. It is as simple as that. No human protection is needed for the royal heir. Why, then, do you work against me, *Tjaty*?"

Neb looked his captor in the eye and said, "The answer to your question is in the very title that you just pronounced with such contempt. I am the king's vizier, and it is my sworn duty to protect his interests. By taking arms against the royal family, you have made yourself my enemy."

"So be it, then, vizier," said jackal-head, turning his back to Neb. As jackal-head and his two companions walked quickly away, a thin mist began to fill the hall. Neb's vision blurred. The last thing he remembered was a sweet odor of burning incense and a distant sound of music.

Neb awoke to find himself in the open desert. It was still night, but a faint glimmer of light was beginning to show itself in the eastern sky. It would soon be day.

Neb was sitting on a stone bench, facing east. He was still bound at the ankles and wrists. He noted that his golden collar of office and his signet ring had been removed from him. He was all alone, except for a stone statue to his right, a statue in the shape of a squatting lion with the head of a man. This type of statue had only recently been invented, and there were only a few like it in all of Egypt. It was called a sphinx. As the light in the eastern sky continued to grow brighter, Neb tried to see the sphinx's face, but the statue was turned so that he could only make out the left ear and part of the cheek.

"I see you like the sphinx," said a familiar voice to Neb's left.

Neb turned toward the voice. It was jackal-head.

"That's good. You and the sphinx will be spending a long time together. Many centuries, in fact."

Neb looked at jackal-head questioningly, but he didn't say a word.

"Oh, you don't understand," said jackal-head. "How forgetful of me. I didn't tell you about the sphinx."

Neb's anger swelled. He wanted to punish this offensive man who stood before him disguised as one of the great gods of Egypt. If only he could use his magic powers!

"Trying to use your powers again, *Tjaty*? Don't bother. You will never break out of the invisible net in which you are now trapped."

Jackal-head moved closer to Neb. He bent his head and spoke in a low voice, almost in a whisper. "Soon I will begin to recite an incantation. I will cast a spell that will force your soul to leave your body, and I shall imprison your soul in the stone statue that you see before you."

Jackal-head bent still lower. His snout was now almost touching Neb's left ear. His voice was just a faint whisper, but his words cut deeply into Neb's mind. "The sphinx is a creature of great power, and I am sure that in time you will learn to use that power. But, trapped within that hard stone body, your soul will watch the centuries go by. You will not be dead, but not truly alive either."

"What will happen to my body?"

"Oh, you are concerned that your body be preserved as is the custom." Jackal-head paused a moment, as he stood up. He was no longer whispering.

"Your body will be given the proper funeral that your rank deserves. Your mummified remains will be buried in your tomb; no harm will come to them. But you will never be reincarnated: your soul will never be able to reunite with your body in the Western Lands. Your soul will remain imprisoned forever in the sphinx."

"Imprisoned . . . forever." The harsh words bored into Neb's mind, as his lips unwillingly repeated them. *No*, he thought; *not forever. There must be some way out; there always is.*

But jackal-head seemed to read Neb's mind; or maybe he just read the expression on Neb's face. "Oh yes, my *Tjaty*, one more thing I forgot to tell you. There is a chance for your soul to be released from the sphinx some day, but your opportunities for escape will be severely limited. You have been King Djedef-Ra's faithful dog. So let's have your king return a favor to you, *Tjaty*: the spell with which I will now bind you to the sphinx can be broken only when a descendant of King Djedef-Ra rules over Egypt."

Laughing loudly, jackal-head moved away from Neb. He put his right hand into the folds of his flowing gown and withdrew a small vial containing a clear liquid. Then, with a sudden motion, he threw the vial forcefully to the ground in front of Neb.

Smoke rose from the shattered vial and enveloped Neb. Neb's head began to spin, as he heard jackal-head's voice droning through the mist:

O great god Set, god of deserts, god of war. Take this man's soul, and rip it from his body. Let him not be reincarnated; may he not rise from the dead in the Western Lands. Imprison his soul in the cold stone sphinx, that the Benu bird may never come to him.

The words were unfamiliar, but Neb could feel the power of the words — lifting him, tearing his immortal soul from his body. He was breathing rapidly now, in shallow gasps. He felt his mind being clouded by the combined effects of the incantation and the drugs that jackal-head had given him before, and he knew he would be able to remember neither the words of the incantation nor anything else about the magic spell.

Neb felt a dull ache in the depths of his consciousness as his body went limp. For a moment, his soul was free. But the freedom was only an illusion: almost before Neb realized it, the stone walls of the sphinx's body surrounded him.

Jackal-head's voice was just a distant echo now, the words indistinct. Neb felt his soul uniting with the sphinx. Through the sphinx's body, he felt the desert air blowing, stroking him. Looking through the sphinx's eyes, for a moment Neb caught a glimpse of his enemy standing in the vast emptiness of the desert as the sun rose above the horizon. Then jackal-head was gone, and Neb was all alone again.

Neb felt the power of the sphinx surging through every inch of the great stone statue. With that power, someday perhaps he could learn to break the evil spell and free his soul. But it was a power unlike any he had ever known, and he knew it would take him many, many years to learn to use the sphinx's power. He prayed to his gods to give him strength, and wisdom to find the path to freedom. Meanwhile, there was nothing he could do to protect King Djedef-Ra against his jackal-headed enemy. With sorrow in his heart, Neb prepared himself to endure the centuries, awaiting the distant day when, if the gods should favor him, he might be able to break the spell that held him prisoner in the body of the sphinx.

CHAPTER 2

THE SPHINX

Jon gulped down his lunch quickly and asked to go to the bathroom. As he was leaving the lunch room, he gave the teacher a broad smile in his usual easy-going manner.

He had planned everything carefully. During the past week he had already sneaked out of school successfully twice before, but still he was nervous. There was always a chance that something could go wrong. The principal already considered Jon a troublemaker, and if Jon got caught now trying to sneak out of the building without permission — well, Jon didn't even want to think about it. He'd be in really deep trouble then, and it wouldn't even matter who Jon's father was.

Jon looked around. Three of his classmates were down the hall, but they weren't looking in his direction. Instead of going up the stairs, Jon turned the corner quickly and headed towards the back door.

As was usual during lunch hour, Tom, the school's custodian, was guarding the back door. Jon didn't want to attract his attention, so he stopped at a distance from Tom. He didn't look at Tom directly. Instead, Jon pretended he was looking at the pictures on the wall, while he watched the custodian out of the corner of his eye.

Tom sat by the door reading a newspaper. Now and then he looked up. He was wearing his reading glasses, and Jon figured that with those glasses Tom couldn't see him clearly enough to identify him. Jon waited.

"Hey! Give that back to me," somebody down the hall yelled.

Jon turned his head to see what the shouting was all about. Some upper classmen were picking on a freshie. It was rather predictable. Something was always happening, and if you had just a little patience, it wouldn't take too long before something got Tom's attention. Tom went to break up the fight.

Jon saw his chance and quickly walked out the back door. Tom didn't even notice. As soon as Jon was out the door, he looked back to make sure nobody had followed him out. He raised a fist triumphantly, and a whispered shout escaped his lips: "Yes!" Then he ran down the block as fast as he could.

This was the third time in one week that Jon was going to the museum. Ever since Mrs. Gunther, the World History teacher, had taken the class to the museum to see the ancient Egypt exhibit last week, something was drawing Jon, making him return again and again. Because at the museum last week, something strange had happened, something that made no sense at all. And Jon felt he had to get to the bottom of it.

The museum was only one block from Jon's school, but Jon was out of breath by the time he got there. Still, he couldn't stop even for a moment. He didn't have much time till his next class, and later today he had an important basketball game. He ran up the stone stairs and entered the building.

As always, the great hall was filled with people. Jon turned right, snaking his way around all the people as he headed towards the entrance to the Egyptian section.

The large stone statue of a squatting lion with a man's head stood guard at the entrance to the Egyptian section, and Jon stopped to read the information card describing the statue. "SPHINX," the card said. Jon already knew the rest by heart, but he kept on reading anyway:

> "This sphinx, made of limestone, was found in front
> of a temple built by King Djedef-Ra (2566-2558 BCE).
> Sphinxes generally had the face of a king or queen. But
> the face of this sphinx is not that of King Djedef-Ra or
> of any known king. The face is still unidentified."

Jon stood and looked at the sphinx. He remembered his trip to the museum last week with the class.

"The Egyptians believed the sphinx had magic powers," Mrs. Gunther had told the class. "And with his powers, this sphinx guarded the king's temple."

"What kind of magic powers?" somebody had asked.

Mrs. Gunther hesitated a moment and said, "That's a very good question, Peter. Maybe you'd like to do a report on it."

Jon found the sphinx fascinating. He walked around the sphinx, studying its shape. He looked into the statue's eyes, trying to imagine what type of magic the Egyptians believed it had. And then he thought he saw the statue blink.

At first, Jon thought his imagination was playing tricks on him. How could a statue blink? It was made of stone. And yet, he was almost sure he had seen it blink.

He stopped and quickly turned around, as if to catch the sphinx off guard. He took a long look at the sphinx, staring into its eyes again. But the statue just sat there, looking at nobody in particular, just as it had been doing for the last four and a half thousand years.

Jon looked around at his friends. Nobody else in the class seemed to have noticed anything unusual. *I must have imagined it,* Jon had decided. The sphinx couldn't possibly have blinked.

The class had moved on to see the mummies, just past the sphinx, and Jon hurried to keep up with the class. One of the girls was trying to peek through a small crack in a mummy case.

"Is there really a dead body in there?" she asked, wrinkling her nose.

"Yeah, I think so," said Jon.

"It's not real, is it?"

"Of course it's real!" Jon answered.

The girl wrinkled her nose again. "Why don't they let you see it?"

"The body is all wrapped up in cloth inside the case," said Mrs. Gunther. "The face on the mummy case is a painting of the person inside. This one was a queen."

The girl circled the mummy case while Mrs. Gunther explained that the ancient Egyptians believed in a life after death. The bodies in the mummy cases were treated with special chemicals so they wouldn't decay, so the soul would be able to enter the body again in the afterlife.

Mrs. Gunther pointed to a painting on the wall. "This painting came from a temple located right near the place where a great king was buried. The painting shows how the king goes down to the Underworld after death."

Mrs. Gunther pointed to the figure of an animal-headed man. "This is Anubis, one of the gods of the Underworld. Here you see him weighing the king's soul to see if the king was good or bad. Other gods are watching Anubis weigh the soul. And a monster with the body of a hippopotamus and the head of a crocodile stands hungrily nearby, waiting to pounce on the king if his soul is judged to be evil."

Out of the corner of his eye, Jon thought he saw something move. He turned to see, just in time. The sphinx had wagged his tail. Actually he had just swished it up and down. Now the tail was back in its place, as before. But Jon had seen it move, and this time he was sure of it. Jon felt his heart racing.

"Were sphinxes ever alive, Mrs. Gunther?" Jon asked.

Mrs. Gunther looked rather surprised at the question. "Of course not, Jon. It's just a statue."

"No, I mean were there ever any living sphinxes? You know, real animals with a person's head and a lion's body?"

"The answer is still no, of course. It was just a myth. Those Egyptians had good imaginations. About as good as your imagination, I think."

The class laughed.

Jon felt sort of foolish and embarrassed now. Mrs. Gunther must be wondering why a fourteen-year-old would ask such a childish question. And yet, Jon knew he had seen the sphinx move.

That was last week. Now, here he was again, for the third time this week. Yesterday and the day before, the sphinx had done nothing out of the ordinary. That is to say, the sphinx had done absolutely nothing. And Jon had returned to school disappointed. Actually, he still couldn't get over the feeling that he had just imagined the sphinx moving and that he was being very childish. But, at the same time, he could feel some kind of power within the sphinx. Jon knew it sounded crazy, but somehow he felt as though the sphinx were trying to tell him something.

Maybe, Jon thought, there was some great secret the sphinx wanted to reveal after all these years. *But why now? And why did he pick me?*

Whispering, he said, "Hey, sphinx. It's me – Jon. Jonathan Travis. I'm back." He looked around to make sure nobody heard him. He felt very foolish talking to a statue.

He stared into the sphinx's eyes, hoping the statue would speak to him.

In an even softer whisper, Jon said, "I saw you move last week."

But the sphinx was silent. Finally, disappointed again, Jon moved away from the statue and went farther into the Egyptian exhibit.

There were statues of kings and queens and gods with heads of different animals. And there were many paintings of scenes of daily life in ancient Egypt. Jon saw his reflection in the glass that protected one of the paintings. He saw himself inside the painting and tried to imagine what it was like to live in those times. He closed his eyes and imagined himself walking in the palace, then running on the burning desert sand. Behind him, in the distance, were the pyramids.

In his mind, the scene shifted. He was no longer running, but standing on a great stone walkway. To either side of him, the emptiness of the desert stretched as far as the eye could see. Behind him stood a single pyramid. In front of him was a great stone temple glittering in the sunlight. And there, standing in front of the temple, was the sphinx with the unknown face.

Jon opened his eyes. *That sure seemed real,* he thought. But now the sand and pyramid and sphinx were gone, and Jon was standing in front of a wooden boat taken from one of the pyramids. It was the boat that was supposed to carry the king's soul to the afterworld following his death.

As he was leaving the Egyptian section, Jon thought he heard a voice calling his name. Actually it was just a loud whisper, but there was no question about it: someone was calling him.

Jon felt a shiver go up his spine. He stopped. He looked toward the whispered voice, but nobody was there. No person, anyway. Just the sphinx with the unknown face.

The sphinx was a popular exhibit, and usually it was surrounded by a small crowd. But strangely, right now not even one person was nearby. And nobody was even looking in that direction.

"Jonathan, come here. There is not much time." The voice seemed to be coming from deep within the lion-like body.

Jon looked at the sphinx. The sphinx had not moved. Not even a blink or a swish of its tail. Not even the slightest movement of the sphinx's stone lips. But there was no question at all in Jon's mind: the sphinx was talking to him.

Sweating and a little bit scared now, Jon moved towards the sphinx again. He didn't say anything. As he moved closer, he just watched the sphinx's face.

But Jon had hesitated too long. Already people were beginning to look in his direction, and others were approaching rapidly. The sphinx was right: there was not enough time for more than a few brief words.

"Return tonight when the moon is full," said the whispered voice. "We will talk then."

Other people were now quite close, and Jon knew the sphinx would say no more. Besides, it was getting late. He had to go. But now he understood that the human-headed lion was more than just a statue. The sphinx had something important to tell him, something that had waited four and a half thousand years to be told. Jon knew he had to return tonight.

He turned, and ran all the way back to school.

CHAPTER 3

THE DOOR

When Jon came home from school that day, he was surprised to see a television news van parked across the street from his house. A uniformed policeman stood at either side of the front door. Neither officer said a word as Jon opened the door.

"Mom," Jon called as he entered the house. Mom was nowhere in sight, and there were voices coming from the den.

"Mom?" he called again.

Mom came running out of the den and signaled Jon to be quiet. "Later," she whispered. "Your father's on the phone with someone important."

Dad was usually not home at dinnertime, but when he was home there was almost always "something important" or "someone important." It seemed to Jon that almost everything was more important than he was.

Mom whispered, "Somebody just tried to assassinate the Egyptian president. Go up to your room. We'll have dinner as soon as Dad gets off the phone."

Jon's father, Congressman Travis, was on all sorts of important government committees. Anytime something big happened anywhere in the world, his father got a call. Jon knew it could be a long time before Dad got off the phone.

Jon went upstairs, annoyed at being rushed off to his room. He threw his knapsack down on the floor next to his bed. He wasn't about to tell his parents about the talking sphinx. Nobody would believe him, so why bother? He slammed his door shut and lay down on his bed.

It wasn't that his parents didn't love him. He knew they did. But they often acted as though he were an inconvenience. Mostly they just ignored him.

Jon turned on his television. Sure enough, the assassination attempt was all over the news:

"Today, only one day after Amir Hassan's inauguration as president of Egypt, a lone gunman fired two shots at him. President Hassan was only slightly injured and is expected to recover. The gunman has not been caught, and no terrorist group has claimed responsibility for the shooting."

Jon had never before been very interested in politics, and he usually found news stories about political leaders rather boring. But now he couldn't tear himself away from the news, and when that broadcast was over he flipped through several other stations searching for more information about the shooting. By the time Jon turned the TV off, he was surprised to find that close to an hour had passed.

At dinner, Dad was really tense. "They don't even want to give the guy a chance. His second day in office, and already they try to kill him!"

"But why?" Jon asked. "Somebody on the news said the gunman was a religious fanatic. Is that right?"

"That's not likely," said Dad. "Don't believe everything you hear on the news."

Dad was about to say something, but Jon interrupted: "What's a Copt? The news said that President Hassan is a Copt."

Dad looked annoyed at the interruption. "Your mother will explain it to you later."

Dad took a bite of his dinner. Then, turning to Mom, Dad continued: "My gut feeling tells me that the shooting has to do with Hassan's tough position on terrorism. Terrorists will have a rough time if Hassan lives up to what he's promised."

There was very little conversation for the rest of dinner. Dad was obviously not in the mood to talk. He gulped down his meal hurriedly, excused himself, and went back to the telephone.

When Dad had left the kitchen, Jon again asked Mom about the Copts.

"Copts claim to be descendants of the pharaohs," Mom said.

Jon thought that over for a few seconds. Other questions came to his mind, but Mom also didn't seem in the mood to talk, so he finished his dinner silently and went up to his room to do his homework.

Tonight he had less homework than usual, and it was rather easy. Which was just as well, since he was having trouble keeping his mind focused on his work. He kept thinking about the sphinx and about ancient Egypt. And about President Hassan, who descended from the pharaohs. He wondered which pharaoh might have been the president's ancestor.

There was one more thing that trouble Jon. Why did the president of Egypt get shot today, the very day that the sphinx spoke after centuries of silence? It seemed too unlikely to be just a coincidence.

Jon finished his homework and looked out the window at the moon.

"Return tonight when the moon is full," the sphinx had said this afternoon. Now it was time, and Jon could hardly wait to find out what the sphinx wanted to tell him. But he couldn't go yet, not till Mom was in her room asleep.

It seemed forever, but it was less than an hour later that Mom finally went upstairs, kissed Jon goodnight, and went to her room. Jon waited another twenty minutes. He opened the door of his room and tiptoed slowly down the stairs.

Dad was still in his study, talking on the phone. Jon could hear his father's voice booming through the closed door of the study. Jon listened, trying to hear what Dad was saying. He stepped on the bottom step, and it squeaked as he put his weight on it.

"Is that you, Jon?" his father called from the study.

Jon didn't answer. He froze in place and held his breath. He waited.

"Jon?"

For a moment, he thought of running back up the stairs. But just as he was about to do so, he quickly changed his mind: Dad would surely hear him going up the stairs. He decided to stay where he was, on the bottom step.

It seemed like a long time, but finally his father returned to his telephone conversation again. Carefully, listening to make sure his father was still talking on the phone, Jon descended the last step.

Another thought occurred to Jon: what if Dad looks for him after he finishes his phone call? Maybe it would be best to go back upstairs and wait until Dad goes to bed. But that could be a long time. And besides, Dad hardly seemed to pay much attention to Jon normally. Tonight, with all that was going on, Jon was pretty sure Dad wouldn't notice his absence. He decided to go ahead.

Tiptoeing, he hurried through the kitchen and the mudroom to the back door. Cautiously, he opened the back door, making sure it didn't squeak. Then he went out and gently closed the door behind him.

Whew, that was close! he thought.

When he got to the street corner, he hesitated. The street light on that corner wasn't working: the red light just flickered on for a few seconds every so often and then went off again, as if warning Jon of danger ahead.

Mom and Dad will kill me if they find out I'm roaming around the city in the middle of the night.

Jon looked up and down the street. There wasn't anybody in sight. He was all alone. He knew it wasn't such a good idea for him to go to the museum now after all. Maybe he should just go back to the house and forget all about it. Or maybe he could go back to the museum this weekend.

But that's not what the sphinx had told him to do. The sphinx had said tonight, when the moon is full. Somehow Jon felt the sphinx's powers would protect him from harm. He started to run.

Jon's house was a few blocks from the museum, and he ran all the way. So by the time he reached the museum he was all out of breath. He stood by the front entrance for a moment, panting. He looked around, making sure nobody was around to see him. Finally he tried to open the door. It was locked. There were two smaller doors on either side of the main door. He tried both of them, but they were also locked.

Jon felt cheated. He had been sure one of the doors would be open. With his magic, the sphinx should have unlocked a door for him. Jon couldn't imagine what had gone wrong. Didn't the sphinx want to talk to him tonight? No, not just *want*. *Need*! The sphinx *needed* to talk to Jon tonight, didn't he? The sphinx had waited for thousands of years, but he couldn't wait a day longer. Jon knew it had to be tonight.

He tried the door again. It was still locked. Slowly, dejectedly, he began to walk away. But after a few paces, he stopped abruptly. He mustn't give up! The sphinx was counting on him. There must be a way in after all, and he would just have to find it.

He went around to the back door. The museum was large, and so it took a while to go around to the back. Jon was scared walking alone on the dark street. And, to make matters worse, the rear of the museum bordered on a park. Jon had to walk along a deserted dirt path to reach the back door.

Jon turned left as he rounded the rear corner of the building. Now he could no longer see the street lights, and it was almost completely dark. He had only the light of the full moon to guide him.

In the park to his right, an owl hooted. Jon thought the sound had come from a nearby tree. He looked in that direction, his eyes trying to adjust to the darkness. Again the owl hooted, but Jon could not see the owl.

A shadow raced from left to right across the path in front of him and disappeared into the park. Trembling, Jon looked around. A pair of eyes stared at him from the darkness to his right. Jon stared back, trying to stay calm, trying not to turn and run. The eyes continued staring at him. Then suddenly they vanished without a sound. It could have been just a cat, but Jon didn't think so.

He began to walk forward again slowly. Behind him, he heard leaves rustling just off the path. He looked back. Nothing. Only darkness.

But he knew it wasn't nothing. He knew he felt a presence. Something was there in the darkness watching him.

Maybe it wasn't such a good idea coming here at night after all. But he was here already, and the back door was just a short distance ahead. He began to run.

He didn't stop to look around but ran straight to the door and tried the knob. It was locked. He couldn't believe it. Again he tried to open the door, but there was no mistake about it: the back door, too, was locked.

Disappointed and scared, he returned to the path and continued walking, keeping the building to his left. To his right, he still felt eyes watching him, although he couldn't see them in the darkness.

He figured he should just go home. But before giving up, he decided to try the front door again, to be completely sure. At least the front door faced the street, and he didn't think the eyes would follow him there. He started walking faster.

As he was walking around the other side of the museum, suddenly he noticed another door. The building curved a little here, and the side door was not along the main path. Jon thought he was very lucky to have seen it in the dark. He wasn't sure whether he had ever known about this entrance before, although he supposed that probably he had known about it and had just forgotten.

He approached the side entrance slowly, looking around to see if anything was lurking in the bushes. This door didn't look as if it was meant to be used by the public. It was probably a delivery entrance, Jon thought.

He put his hand on the doorknob, looked around again to make sure nobody was following him, and turned the knob.

CHAPTER 4

THE MUSEUM

The door opened!

Jon walked slowly through the darkened hallway, his eyes darting in all directions, his outstretched hands groping in the dim light. He wasn't sure exactly in what part of the museum he was. Nothing looked familiar. There were no exhibits here, and no signs either.

As he turned a corner, for a moment he feared that something evil lurked beyond. His breath caught in his throat, and all his muscles tensed.

It sure is scary here, he thought. For a minute he even wondered whether he was in the museum at all. Maybe the door through which he had entered was not an entrance to the museum after all.

Then, up ahead, he saw a staircase and a sign: "To Exhibits." He breathed a sigh of relief and ran up the stairs.

No sooner had Jon reached the top of the stairs than he heard the sound of footsteps. A museum guard was coming.

"Who's there?" the guard demanded.

I can't get caught. I have to get to the sphinx. Jon crept away from the stairs and hid in a dark corner nearby.

The guard was still coming towards him, shining a flashlight left and right. The guard stopped and looked down the stairs. He went down three steps, paused, looked down the side of the bannister, and returned to the top of the staircase. He looked to his right and to his left, and finally he shone the light toward the corner where Jon was hiding.

Jon pressed himself against the wall of the little corner, just barely outside the beam of light. He froze. He didn't even dare to breathe. For now, the curve of the wall shielded him from the light. If the guard were to move just two or three steps to his side, he would be able to catch Jon with the flashlight beam. Fortunately, however, the guard did not move to the side. After what seemed a very long time, the guard turned the flashlight away and went down the stairs.

That was close, Jon thought.

He got up and looked around. Nobody was there. But he knew he didn't have much time before the guard would come back up the stairs. He had to go on.

Jon started to walk down the main hallway. This time, he was much more careful not to make any noise. As he walked, he kept looking all around, watching for museum guards.

The passageway now seemed familiar. He still wasn't sure exactly where he was, but at least he knew he was heading in the right direction. All he had to do was to keep on going, and make sure the guards didn't catch him.

Up ahead there was a light. Jon hurried in that direction. The passageway widened, and he was now in the hall of Knights in Armor. The walls were lined with displays of swords and spears and suits of metal armor. In the middle of the hall, two knights sat on armor-covered horses facing each other, each knight holding a long lance pointing forward at the other knight. Jon loved this exhibit, and he stopped just a moment to look. He had visited this exhibit many times before, but now for the first time he noticed how short the knights must have been to fit into those suits of armor.

He left the Knights in Armor and hurried down the narrow corridor to his left. Now he knew exactly where he was. He didn't have far to go to reach the sphinx.

"Who goes there?" The deep voice echoed through the corridor, and Jon wasn't sure from which direction it had come. He glanced to either side, looking for guards. He froze in place, too scared to move.

"You are on forbidden ground," the voice said. "Turn back immediately!"

As the warning echoed in his ears, Jon knew it was not a guard who had just spoken. He looked around again. He saw nobody, and that scared him even more. He almost turned back. But then he thought of the sphinx waiting for him with his secret of thousands of years. He knew that the secret, whatever it was, could no longer wait even one more day; it had to be told tonight. He gathered up his courage and started walking forward.

A shadow streaked across the wall to Jon's right. Jon felt it go by, but by the time he looked, the shadow was gone. He ducked his head, although he couldn't say why. He looked up. There was nothing unusual above him.

Slowly, cautiously, he began again to inch forward.

Again, the shadow raced across the wall. Jon heard a rush of wind, as though a bird had just flown by. He looked up but saw nothing. Maybe it wasn't a bird, after all; maybe it was a bat.

Suddenly the corridor was plunged into darkness. He stopped and listened.

Nothing. Only darkness. And the sound of his own beating heart.

There was a faint light up ahead in the distance. Jon again started walking, trying not to touch any of the exhibits that lined the walls. His eyes darted in all directions, trying to probe the darkness. Every few steps, he stopped to listen for the sound of footsteps following him. But there were no footsteps, other than his own.

Suddenly, he felt the presence of another person. He stopped.

"Who's there?" he whispered, almost to himself.

There was no answer.

Again he heard the sound of something up above, something coming towards him from the ceiling. He looked up.

The air above him seemed heavy, and he thought he could see the suggestion of a human form. He stared at the shape and tried to focus. Gradually the outlines became more clear. It was the head and upper body of a woman suspended in mid-air. Around her neck, she wore a golden necklace. Her eyes were outlined in black. Her lips were painted red. Her dark hair, ornamented with fine gold chains, hung over her shoulders in front of her. Her face was both beautiful and incredibly powerful. There was no doubt about it: this was an Egyptian queen.

"Go back!" said the woman. "Do not attempt to meddle in affairs that don't concern you."

Jon tried to answer, but his words caught in his throat. He tried again, and this time, somehow, he was able to get the words out of his mouth. "I must go on. The sphinx sent for me."

The woman laughed loudly. The walls echoed with her sarcastic laughter, and Jon could even see her golden necklace vibrating with the sound. She looked directly at Jon and said, "Do not listen to the sphinx. His way will lead to death. Turn back, I say. You have been warned."

The woman's image faded, and all was dark again. He no longer felt her presence, but he knew she still was watching him, waiting to see what he would do. The woman's threat had shaken him, but somehow he was able to suppress his fear. Even if his parents and his teachers had never believed in him, Jon felt a certain determination. There was no doubt in his mind that he had to go on, despite the woman's threat. Somehow, he'd reach the sphinx, no matter what!

In the darkness, Jon heard a growling sound. At first, the growling was very low, and he had to strain to hear it. But soon it grew louder and seemed to surround Jon. He looked in all directions, trying to see where the sound was coming from. It sounded as if a pack of wolf-like animals were encircling him, closing in on him, their jaws open, their large teeth dripping blood. Again he looked this way and that. He wanted to run, but he didn't know in which direction to go.

And then he saw it: a man with an animal's furry face and a long snout. It was a jackal's head, and it was coming towards him. The jackal's long snout opened, revealing its sharp teeth. The human body faded away, and a jackal's body took its place. The jaws snapped open and shut, as the eyes looked hungrily at Jon.

Jon started to run, back in the direction from which he had come. He did not look back. Behind him he heard the growling and the snarling as the jackal chased him down the long corridor, getting closer, ever closer.

A light shone in the distance, and Jon ran towards the light, dodging exhibits as he went. The jackal was now almost on top of him. He heard the jackal's breathing just behind his left ear, and he even thought he felt the animal's warm breath on the back of his neck.

With a scream, Jon fell to the floor, crawled under a table, quickly rose to his feet at the other side of the table, and, reversing his direction, started to run again down the corridor towards the sphinx.

Jon ran as fast as he could, but he was getting tired and was almost out of breath. Behind him he heard the patter of the jackal's feet on the marble floor. Jon's dodge under the table had put some additional distance between him and the jackal, but the animal was again narrowing the distance rapidly, and Jon knew he wouldn't be able to outrun the jackal for long.

Ahead and somewhat to the right, the royal lady again was floating in mid-air, a wicked smile on her face. "You were warned!" she said, her right hand pointing at Jon.

Jon tried his best not to look at the queen. He had to give all his attention to running forward along the dark and narrow corridor which, he knew, would soon end as it joined the great hall where the sphinx stood waiting. But there was nothing he could do to avoid looking at the terrifying object that suddenly appeared in front of him: a mummy's coffin with Jon's face painted on it.

The coffin hung in the air, in the distance at the end of the corridor. The coffin's lid opened, revealing only an endless, gaping pit inside, as it waited for Jon's body to fill its emptiness. Behind him, the royal lady laughed loudly, while the jackal's pattering footsteps rapidly approached, their sound echoing in Jon's ears.

As Jon neared the end of the corridor, he saw that the coffin was standing just before the entrance into the great hall, blocking his way. The jackal was almost at his heels. Jon was trapped.

The jackal sprang into the air, straight at Jon. But somehow, Jon sensed the jackal's movement just as it was beginning its jump. Jon quickly fell to the floor, and he heard the rush of air above him as the animal hurtled past, narrowly missing him.

The jackal scrambled to its feet, preparing to attack again. Jon was still on the floor, face down. As he rose, he knew there was nothing more he could do. His eyes locked with the jackal's eyes, trying to stare the animal down, but knowing that was hopeless. The jackal bared its teeth and snarled. Any moment he would strike. In the background, Jon heard the queen's victorious laughter. He hardly heard the sound of the wind that was gathering above him.

But the jackal heard. The jackal closed his mouth, twitched his ears, and nervously sniffed the air. He turned his eyes away from Jon and listened to the ever-increasing sound of the wind that whirled above Jon's head. Too late, the jackal realized his danger and began to run away.

Jon watched the wind strike the coffin with all its force, seizing it and smashing it against the wall. Suddenly Jon felt the wind suck him up, lifting him off the ground. Unable to gain a foothold, he tumbled over as he was swept forward towards the corridor's end.

The wind pounded hard against the jackal, hurling him back through the dark corridor, away from Jon. Even the queen could not resist the wind. Her laughter stopped abruptly, and her image trembled as she was driven backwards by the angry wind. She raised her voice in a terrible, piercing scream as she disappeared with the jackal into the darkness.

CHAPTER 5

NEB

Jon found himself lying sprawled on the floor in the middle of the hall. Behind him was the museum's main entrance, and the outside world. In front of him and far to his left was the darkened corridor from which he had just come. Fearfully, he looked in that direction, half expecting a jackal or an even more ferocious beast to come charging towards him. Slowly he rose to his feet, breathing heavily, his eyes still fixed on the darkened corridor. He waited, but no beast or spirit came out of the darkness to attack him.

Jon felt he was being watched. His eyes darted in all directions, catching quick glimpses of his surroundings. He saw nobody.

The hall where Jon now stood was familiar to him, and yet it seemed very different in the dim light and without the crowds that were always present during the day. To his right was the Egyptian section. Slowly, cautiously, he began to walk in that direction, squinting in the semi-darkness, straining to see. As he walked forward, he felt the sphinx's power drawing him, growing ever stronger as he approached the sphinx.

All at once, out of the darkness the sphinx came into view, glowing faintly in the dark, waiting silently just as he had been doing for the last four and a half thousand years. And, Jon knew, the sphinx was waiting for him.

Jon felt his heart racing. He could hardly wait to hear the sphinx's secret. Quickly, his eyes scanned the hall, making sure no guards or ancient spirits were in sight. Then he ran straight to the sphinx as quickly as his legs would carry him.

Excitedly, he came to a halt next to the great stone statue. He stood in front of the sphinx, looking into its cold, lifeless limestone eyes. The sphinx was silent.

Jon wasn't sure why the sphinx wasn't talking to him. Wasn't he eager to tell his tale? Maybe he was just waiting for Jon to speak first.

"I'm here," Jon said. "I came, just as you asked me to. They tried to stop me, but I made it anyway."

The stone eyes stared blankly. The eyelids didn't blink. The lips did not move. But from deep within the statue, a voice rose up.

"My name is Neb. I have waited many years for you. I thank you for coming."

"Huh?"

"I said, my name is Neb," said the statue. "When I was alive, I was the king's vizier."

Jon could hardly believe his ears. All these years, this sphinx's identity had been a mystery. Even the greatest Egyptologists didn't know its identity; but now, Jon, a fourteen-year-old kid, knew the sphinx's name. A smile broke out over Jon's face.

"No way!" said Jon.

"What did you say?"

"I said, 'No way.' I mean, that's really great. And I'm very pleased to meet you, Neb. But what's a vizier?"

Now the statue blinked. It seemed he was surprised that anybody would not know what a vizier was.

"Why, the vizier is the king's chief minister. After the king, I was the most powerful man in all of Egypt. And I was a magician of great power. But even all my powers couldn't save me from my fate."

Jon's eyes opened wide. "What happened to you, Neb?"

The sphinx continued to stare ahead. His stone face didn't change. And yet, Jon could feel a certain sadness in the sphinx's voice as he answered.

"I was poisoned," said the sphinx. "It was a rare and powerful poison known as *metut An*. My assassin killed my body, and, using magic, he trapped my *ka* — that is my soul — inside this sphinx."

Jon's mouth opened, but for a moment he couldn't speak. He had expected the sphinx to tell him a dark and terrible tale. In fact, Jon had sort of suspected it would be a tale of murder. But hearing it now, straight from the sphinx's mouth, it was a surprise to him anyway.

In a shaky voice, Jon asked, "Did you see who did it?"

The sphinx's stony eyelids seemed to droop. "He was disguised as the god Anubis. He wore a jackal mask. I couldn't see his face. But I have my suspicions. Anyway, I can't tell you any more about that right now. You must have patience. You will learn all, in time. For now, just listen carefully. Then I will need to know whether you will help me."

"Of course I'll help you, if I can," Jon said. "That's why I came tonight, isn't it?"

The sphinx's lips seemed to curl up a bit, and Jon thought he saw a trace of a smile on the stone face.

"Yes, Jonathan. Of course I know you want to help me. But that is not the reason you have come tonight: you came because you were curious, but you don't really understand yet what helping me involves. First hear my story; then you can tell me whether you will help. Have you ever heard of King Djedef-Ra?"

Jon was about to shake his head, but then he remembered. "Sure I've heard of him. He's the king on that card there." Jon pointed to the information card in front of the sphinx. "The card says you were found in front of a temple that he built."

"That is correct, Jonathan. Most people today have never heard of King Djedef-Ra, because his reign was short: only eight years. He didn't manage to do all the things he wanted to do. But still, he was a great king, and I was proud to be his vizier."

"Why was he king for only eight years? What happened to him?"

"Even today, nobody knows," said the sphinx sadly. "He died just a few months after me, while still a young man. Two of his three sons were assassinated shortly before me, and I was investigating their deaths. The investigation was difficult, and I thought I was still very far from solving the crime. But apparently the murderer thought I was getting close, and so he had me eliminated."

"What happened after you died? Did your murderer kill the king?"

"I have only incomplete knowledge of the events that occurred in the few months following my death, and I do not know the exact circumstances of King Djedef-Ra's untimely death. The king had one remaining son, Baka, who should have been king after him. But history tells that when Djedef-Ra died, his brother succeeded him. Nobody knows what happened to Baka, and I fear that both he and King Djedef-Ra met a violent end."

A thought struck Jon. And it was such an obvious thought, he couldn't believe he hadn't thought of it right away.

"Hey, wait a minute, Neb! Something just doesn't make any sense. This all happened a long time ago. Whoever poisoned you is long dead. What can you do about it now, and how could I possibly help you?"

"Ah, Jonathan," said the sphinx. "You have so much to learn. I did not say I could prevent my murder. You are quite correct: I can't do that. However, there are certain things I can do. As I told you, even when I was a living man, I always had magic powers; but since I became a sphinx my magic powers have grown. I can take us back in time."

Jon's jaw dropped, and his eyes opened wide. "Wow! You mean you can take us back to ancient Egypt? Four and a half thousand years, just like that?"

"Yes," said Neb. "Just like that. And in fact, I have gone back a few times, but I was unable to discover anything. I am now a sphinx, and I can't take human form. That's why I need you if I am to find my murderer."

Again, Jon was puzzled. "Why do you need to find the murderer, Neb? You said you can't prevent your murder anyway. So what's the point? Revenge?"

"Yes, revenge would certainly be satisfying, although I'd rather call it bringing a criminal to justice. However, that is not my purpose now. As I said before, my purpose is to free my soul from its imprisonment in the sphinx and then return to ancient Egypt so my soul can unite with my body in the afterlife. But I have been unable to find out the nature of the magic spell that binds me to this statue, and I believe that only after I have found my murderer will I discover how to gain my freedom."

Jon wrinkled his brow. "Something still doesn't make sense. If you can go back in time, why can't you just go back to the time of your murder and follow the man in the jackal mask? Eventually he'd have to take the mask off. Then you'd see his face."

"Yes, I also thought of that," said Neb. "It's rather obvious, isn't it? But it can't be done. It seems I can't go back to any time within a day or two before my death. And even after my assassination, there are certain times to which I cannot go. I have no trouble reaching other times and places: a hundred years ago, five hundred, or a thousand; Europe, India, China. I have been to all of those. But any time and place connected to my death is not within my reach."

"OK," said Jon. "So we go back in time, and you need me to do things for you, because you can't take a human form. But why me? I mean, in all these thousands of years, why couldn't you find anybody else?"

The sphinx's face somehow took on a different appearance now, and his lion-like body shifted slightly. He appeared to be listening for something in the distance, like a lion alert to the sounds of the jungle. Just as before, Neb's voice rose up from the depths of the statue, and Jon shuddered as he spoke.

"I have seen you in my visions, Jonathan. I recognized you when you first came to the museum. My visions show me only bits and pieces, possibilities of what may be. I do not know for sure that you can help me. Perhaps my *ka* is doomed to be imprisoned in this sphinx forever, unable to discover my assassin, unable to prevent the death of Baka and of Djedef-Ra. But this I do know: if there is any chance at all of my success, any chance to free my soul, it lies with you."

The sphinx's face and body seemed to relax, and his voice returned to normal as he continued. "If you decide to go with me to ancient Egypt, I will do my best to protect you with my magic. But remember, Jonathan, we are dealing with a murderer. Now tell me: do you still want to help? Will you go with me?"

Jon didn't wait to be asked again. "Sure!" he said.

And maybe ordinarily Jon wouldn't have agreed to go. Catching a murderer hardly seemed like a job for a fourteen-year-old kid. But these were hardly ordinary circumstances. And, with the sphinx's magic protecting him, Jon thought he would be safe.

"Alright, then," said Neb. "Climb on my back, and we'll be off."

Jon hesitated. "Neb, how long will we be gone?" he asked. In a somewhat lower voice, he added, "Will my parents miss me?"

"As long as my soul is trapped within this sphinx, I must always return to the time and place from which I left. It will be as if no time has passed at all, and no one will notice that you were gone. Now hurry! There is no time."

Jon scrambled up.

"Are you ready, Jonathan?" asked Neb.

"Well, sort of." Jon squirmed around trying to find a comfortable position. It wasn't easy sitting on the hard stone surface. He was trying to find just the right position so he wouldn't slide off the sphinx's smooth, curved back.

Just then, Jon noticed a guard coming. He was still far away, coming out of the Ancient Greece exhibit at the other end of the great hall. He didn't seem to have spotted Jon yet, but he was heading in Jon's direction.

"Quick, Neb!" said Jon. "We have to get out of here before the guard sees us."

The sphinx swished his tail. His ears twitched slightly. He arched his back and began to rise. He was still a statue, but he seemed to be coming alive.

The guard was heading in their general direction, but he wasn't looking directly at the sphinx. Then, out of the corner of his eye, the guard seemed to have seen something move. He looked toward the sphinx. The hall was large, and Jon knew the guard was still not close enough to see exactly what was happening in the dim light. And the sphinx's head hid Jon from the guard's view.

"Come on, Neb!" said Jon. He wrapped his arms around the sphinx's neck and held on to the smooth stone as tightly as he could.

The guard had moved, and now he was looking straight at Jon.

The guard unfastened his holster and drew his gun. He began to run towards the sphinx. "Freeze right there!" he shouted.

Jon froze. He would have done so even had the guard not commanded it. His hands felt cold and clammy, and he was sweating all over. He wanted to tell Neb to do something fast, but he was so scared that he couldn't even talk.

Suddenly, the statue shuddered. It was not just a little shiver, but a mighty, rapid swaying to and fro. Jon felt the statue rising quickly into the air. His vision blurred, and everything became dark.

In the distance, Jon heard the guard shouting something, but the voice rapidly became still more distant and soon faded away completely.

There was silence, a silence deeper than Jon had experienced ever before. In the darkness, lights flickered, like stars in the sky. But Jon knew they were not stars, and the darkness he saw was not the night sky. He was traveling through time, backwards into the long forgotten past.

It was a strange and scary feeling: as if his mind were no longer inside his body. In fact, he wasn't sure just where his body was. He couldn't move his arms or legs. But what scared him most was that he wasn't even breathing, and he couldn't breathe even when he tried. Then his mind became fuzzy, and he remembered nothing more of his trip through time.

CHAPTER 6

EGYPT

Jon opened his eyes. All around him there was sand, stretching for many miles in every direction. The sun's heat beat down on his head. A desert wind pounded at his face and filled his lungs with its hot breath. Even sitting high up on the sphinx's back, he could see and feel the heat rising from the sun-baked sand.

Jon dismounted and looked around. He could hardly believe it. In fact, it seemed impossible that a stone statue could have brought him back in time to ancient Egypt. It seemed crazy. But here he was. Or was he? Maybe he was hallucinating, or dreaming.

"No, Jonathan," said the sphinx. "You are not dreaming. This is real."

Jon spun around quickly and faced the sphinx. "How did you know what I was thinking? Can you read my mind?"

"No, Jonathan, I didn't have to. And I can't anyway. You were whispering, talking to yourself. That is a habit you will have to break very soon. You must not let anyone overhear your thoughts, or you may put yourself in danger. Now climb on my back again, and I will take you to the palace."

The sphinx rose. He straightened first his hind legs, then his front legs, until he was standing majestically on all fours. He turned his head, looking this way and that, like a lion hunting his prey. Jon put his hand on the sphinx's neck. It was still made of stone. And yet, the sphinx's bearing made him seem no longer like the limestone statue that Jon had seen in the museum, but a living, breathing being: half man, half lion.

The sphinx continued to look in all directions. He sniffed at the desert air. He twitched his ears. Slowly he began to move forward, with his hind end raised and his head low, like a lion about to attack.

And Jon was sitting on the lion's back. Jon shuddered at the thought. The sphinx's back was still as hard as stone, and the sphinx's color was still a whitish gray. But the hairs of his mane, no longer made of stone, fluttered in the desert wind. Jon couldn't see the sphinx's face now from where he was sitting. Was it still a man's face? Or was the statue changing completely into a lion?

"Neb?" Jon's voice was trembling.

The sphinx didn't answer. Instead, he suddenly sprang forward and began to run.

The lion raced across the desert. The hot wind sprayed sand in Jon's face, so that he could hardly see what lay ahead of them. He didn't try to talk to Neb again. He just held on tightly to the lion's flowing mane and struggled to keep his balance on the great beast's back.

After a long time — Jon wasn't sure just how long — the lion began to slow down. Jon wiped sand from his face and blinked a few times. It was no longer difficult to keep his balance on the sphinx's back, and so he let go of the mane.

He looked up, beyond the sphinx's head. A short distance ahead, there stood a row of tall stone columns. In front of the columns, two stone sphinxes stood facing the desert, keeping watch. And beyond the row of columns Jon saw a great city surrounded by a white wall.

Neb came to a halt and turned his head. For a moment Jon froze, not knowing quite what to expect. He half expected to see a lion's face and to be eaten alive before he could manage to escape. But it was Neb's face after all.

Neb twitched his ears. "That is the great city of Memphis, where King Djedef-Ra lives."

"And the murderer too, I suppose."

"Yes, it is likely. But we will speak of that later. Right now, I must take you to the palace. Then you will begin to understand."

Jon wanted to ask, "Understand what?" But he knew there was no point in asking. The sphinx would tell him when he thought the time was right, and no sooner. Besides, Neb had already turned his head away from Jon and was again moving onward towards the great white wall.

Neb entered the city at a slow walk, with his head held high and his tail swishing back and forth. Around them, people filled the streets, talking to each other and going about their daily lives. Nobody seemed to notice the walking sphinx or the boy riding on his back.

"I have made us invisible," Neb whispered when no one else seemed to be close by. Again, Neb seemed to have read Jon's unspoken thoughts.

"Cool! I didn't know you could do that. When did we become invisible?"

"Just before we entered the city," Neb answered. "As long as you are on my back, I can make you invisible too. But it takes a lot of energy to maintain the cloak of invisibility, and I can't remain invisible for very long or when I am in rapid motion. Also, indoors the invisibility is only partial. Now be silent: people are approaching."

Suddenly, the streets were filled with people: some running, some walking, but all of them seeming very excited. From far down the street, a great cheer rose up. The sounds of drums and marching feet were heard. The crowds parted, leaving a clear path in the middle of the street.

Six drummers walked in step, beating their drums and chanting in a loud sing-song: "Make way, make way. The king's daughter comes."

The language was one that Jon had never heard before, but surprisingly he found he was able to understand it.

"What language are they speaking?" he asked.

Neb turned to Jon and smiled. "That is the language of ancient Egypt. In your time, no one speaks it any more. With my powers, I have made you able to understand and speak the language as though you were Egyptian."

Behind the drummers, a column of soldiers marched in battle dress, their armor glistening in the sunlight. After the soldiers came a group of four men, naked from the waist up. On their shoulders they carried a sedan chair, and on the chair sat the princess.

Jon strained to see, but the pressing crowd prevented him from getting a good view.

Neb said, "That is the king's stepdaughter. She is the daughter of King Djedef-Ra's second wife. She is a great favorite among the people, and Prince Baka will marry her someday. Her name is Meres-ankh."

Neb began to move away from the crowd.

"Hey!" Jon blurted out. "Can't we stay and watch?"

But Neb kept moving. "We must reach the palace while everyone is still outside watching the procession. Indoors, I am only partially invisible, and the fewer the people whom we encounter there, the smaller is our chance of being seen."

Neb entered the palace by a side entrance and quickly turned off the main corridor. Several times he had to hide in a darkened corner to avoid being noticed by people passing by. Finally he turned into a little-used hallway. After a short distance, they came to a dead end, and Neb told Jon to dismount.

"Over there," Neb said. "There are two torches mounted on the wall. Take one of them, and bring it here."

Jon brought the torch.

"Now bend down, and put your hand into that crevice in the rock."

Jon did so. All he felt was empty space.

"Put your hand in farther," Neb commanded. "As far as you can reach."

Jon hesitated, afraid something in the darkness would jump out and bite him.

"Go on," said Neb. "Don't be afraid. There is a handle deep inside the rock. Pull on it."

Jon reached in, almost to his shoulder. He felt a handle up against the rock. He pulled, but nothing happened.

"You will have to pull harder than that," said Neb. "Give it all your strength."

He did, and the crevice opened, revealing a hidden doorway in the rocky wall.

Quickly they entered the passageway beyond the door. At Neb's direction, Jon found another handle in the rock and pulled the door shut behind them.

Jon held the torch high above his head, trying to see what lay ahead. The passageway was straight and very long.

"Where are we? And where are we going?" he asked, climbing back onto the sphinx's back.

"This is a secret passageway," Neb answered, "known only to the king's most trusted servants. The palace has many secret passageways. This one leads to the room where Prince Baka is hidden."

"So I'm going to meet the prince?"

"Yes," said Neb. "Prince Baka's attempted assassination appeared to be an accident. But the king had his doubts, and he thought it better to hide the prince until he recovers from his injuries. We are almost there. When you meet Prince Baka, it will be clear to you how you can help me."

The sphinx went quickly through the passageway, sloping downward. Twice the way forked, and each time Neb chose the path to the right.

Neb's pace slowed a bit, and he said, "When you enter Prince Baka's chamber, you will need to speak a password. Say, 'Anuk pa ba.'"

In a whisper, Jon repeated the password to himself: "Anuk pa ba."

Soon the passageway leveled, and Neb stopped in front of a large wooden door.

"Open the door."

Jon dismounted and did as he was told, holding the torch before him as he entered the room. Within the room, a soldier stood guard, his sword drawn.

Jon hesitated.

The soldier advanced, his sharp sword pointed at Jon's chest.

In a raspy voice, Jon said, "Anuk pa ba."

The soldier stopped his advance but did not lower his sword.

"Anuk pa ba," Jon said again, this time louder and more steadily.

The soldier sheathed his sword and stood aside, allowing Jon to enter. Jon put his torch into a slot in the wall and approached the bed where Prince Baka lay.

Prince Baka's bed was surrounded by a thin, translucent curtain. Outside the curtain, a female slave sat to the right of the bed, mixing medicines in a large bowl. Jon went around and approached the bed from the left side. He bent over Baka and whispered in his ear.

Baka, surprised, propped himself up on his elbow, his face turned to his right, away from Jon. "Leave us now," he said to the slave and to the soldier. "When you leave my chamber, turn left and go out of earshot. My visitor must speak to me in private."

The slave got up and went to the door. The soldier seemed unwilling to leave, but Baka motioned to him and nodded his head reassuringly.

"I will be alright. You may go now. My visitor will close the door behind you."

The soldier still appeared uncomfortable about leaving his prince alone with a stranger, but he obeyed and left the room. As Jon went to close the door, Neb entered, almost invisible in the dim light.

Neb went to a corner of the room, hidden from Baka's view. Jon closed the door and turned toward Baka, trying to make out Baka's face in the flickering torchlight. Jon approached the bed slowly, uncertain how to start his conversation with the prince. Baka sat up fully. He looked at Jon, and their eyes met. As Jon looked at Baka's face, he saw the startled expression on the prince's face, mirroring his own astonishment.

Baka looked as though he could have been Jon's twin. Their faces were identical.

CHAPTER 7

THE PRINCE

Jon was the first to recover from the shock, but he couldn't think of what to say that would make any sense to Baka. He couldn't say he was from the far future, brought back in time by a sphinx. He didn't think the prince would believe that. In fact, Jon found it difficult to believe it himself.

"Neb sent me to you," Jon said simply.

"Neb? He's dead. Do you come from across the river of death? Has my time come now too? Are you my *ka*, a spirit sent to lead me away to the Western Lands?" There was no alarm at all in Baka's tone of voice.

"No, Prince Baka, I'm not a spirit, and I have not come to take you to the afterworld. I really don't understand this any more than you. Neb brought me here. Maybe he can explain." Jon turned and gestured to Neb.

Now Baka seemed even more surprised than when he first saw Jon. "So Neb brought you here? The old fox still has magic! Even death didn't take that away from him. Where is he? Let him come and speak to me."

Baka looked around the room. "Neb, where are you? Are you hiding somewhere in my chamber? Or have you learned to make yourself invisible?" Baka laughed.

"Exactly so," said Neb, as he came out of the corner and moved into Baka's view, though still only partially visible.

At first, the sphinx's body had a ghost-like quality, and only a vague suggestion of his form was seen. But as Baka watched in amazement, the air began to shimmer, and the sphinx's form solidified, first the feet and tail, then gradually the body and the head.

When Neb was fully visible, he bowed his head and said, "I am at your service, my prince."

Baka's face glowed with happiness, and he said, "I couldn't have asked for a better gift to cheer me up than seeing my old friend Neb come back from the dead. But why, my father's good vizier, do you come in this disguise?"

"My enemy – the man who killed your brothers – imprisoned my soul inside this sphinx. Four and a half thousand years I waited, until at last this boy appeared. I have brought him back from the future world, and with his help I hope to free my soul."

To Jon's surprise, Baka seemed to accept that explanation with no difficulty at all. But Jon himself was still confused.

"This is impossible," Jon said. "The prince is my twin, but we aren't even related!"

"No, Jonathan, it is not impossible at all. Of all the many millions of people who have lived upon this earth, it should not surprise you that now and then two people look alike."

Jon's face lit up. "Hey, I remember last month I read something in a magazine about a look-alike contest. There were about six or seven people who looked just like some famous rock singer."

"Yes, that's right," said Neb. "But still, when
day at the museum, I felt the gods had sent you
your face alone that struck me, though. Over the
learned to see into the human soul. When I looked
amazed: your *ka* resembles Baka's more than any bro ..er s could."

"That's amazing!"

Neb twitched his ears. "It is," he said. "And so I realized this was
no coincidence but an omen, a divine gift to me, to help me gain my
freedom. For thousands of years I have waited, not knowing how
or when my opportunity would come. But now my path is clear. I
know exactly how I must proceed."

With some difficulty, Baka sat up again. "Do you mean to have
him take my place, then, Neb?"

"Yes. The king wants nobody to know you have been injured.
If people knew about your injuries, there are those who then
would claim that you are not a god and therefore not the rightful
heir to Egypt's throne. Your assassin must believe that he has failed
completely, and therefore you must not appear in public yet until
your injuries are healed. It will be many days before you walk again,
and meanwhile what will people think? Jon will substitute for you,
and everyone will see that Baka is not injured."

Baka still looked skeptical. "How will that help? The murderer
will try again."

"Of course he will," said Neb. "And that is just the point. For
only when I know the murderer's identity will I be able to discover
how to gain my freedom. But no harm will come to Jonathan. I will
protect him."

Baka asked, "Will that be enough? I do not mean to be
discourteous, but remember, Neb, you were not even able to
protect yourself."

"You are right, my prince. And you have spoken boldly, as indeed the future king of Egypt should. I admit there still is danger, but I am no longer as you have known me, Baka. For you, it is but a few short weeks since my body died, but my soul has lived inside this statue now for many centuries, and my powers have increased. My magic now is greater than it ever was in life. But I have no living body any more, and so I need Jon's help. I will weave a magic spell around him, to guard against all enemies."

"And while I pretend to be Prince Baka, you will watch and try to learn the identity of the assassin."

"Yes, that is the plan."

Baka asked, "If you can protect him, couldn't you also protect me?"

"No," said Neb. "I wish I could, but unfortunately I cannot. I am from the future, and I cannot use my powers to protect you, who are in my past."

Neb turned to Jon again and said, "Now Jonathan, in spite of my protective magic, you must be always cautious. My spell will not be able protect you from accidental injury, but only from attack and injury by a weapon or a living foe. And so, there still is danger. Will you still help me, Jonathan?"

Jon hesitated as he considered the risks involved. What if something went wrong and he couldn't get home? Then he would never see his family or his friends again. But he could still change his mind . . . . Or could he? Despite Neb's question, Jon wondered whether it was too late to back out now.

"What if I say no?"

"I cannot force you. I can only hope that you will help me. When I met you in the museum, I could not tell you everything. I had to bring you here, so you would see and understand. But now that you have seen, if you decide you do not want to take the risk, then I will take you home."

"Can I ask a question first?"

The sphinx swished his tail. "Of course," he said. "What is it you would like to know?"

"Do you have any clues? Is there anybody you suspect?"

Neb twitched his ears again as he thought for a moment. "For centuries I have been pondering that question. Many times I have gone over in my mind the events relating to my capture and my death. The man who did this to me is a great magician, and I have been unable to penetrate his disguise. But I do not think he acts alone. Someone else is his accomplice, someone who hates the royal heirs or who would somehow benefit from their deaths."

"Like who?" asked Jon.

Baka said, "I can answer that. It is probably a member of the royal family. My grandfather Khufu had many wives. Djedef-Ra, my father, was the son of one of Khufu's lesser wives. King Khufu chose my father to be his heir, but many of our family are jealous of him and claim that he usurped the throne. Some say he was not worthy and that he tricked my grandfather into making him his heir. If my father were to die without a son, one of my father's brothers would take the throne. So you see, any one of them may be the guilty one."

Jon asked Neb, "Why do you think there was an accomplice? Couldn't one of Baka's uncles be the magician who imprisoned you?"

"I do not think so," Neb answered. "The man who murdered me did not seem to be of royal blood. I felt it in his voice and in his manner. No, he was an upstart, proud in the power that his magic gave him. But there is someone else behind him, and that person is a member of the royal family. Of that I am sure."

Jon suddenly felt his heart pounding. Neb's words made him think of the queen who tried to stop him in the museum, and in his mind he saw her face and heard her wicked laughter. He hated to admit it to himself, but he was scared. He liked to read mystery and adventure novels, and often he used to think it would be fun to do the daring things about which he loved to read. But this was not a story. This was real!

And yet, Neb was quite convincing: Jon's strong resemblance to Baka was no mere coincidence. It was meant to be. Besides, here was Jon's chance to be a real prince, for a while anyway.

Jon looked up at Neb. "I'll do it," he said.

CHAPTER 8

ATTACK

The next day

"**C**ome on, Baka! Look alive," Sekhem shouted. He ran up to Jon and said, "You don't seem to be yourself today. Did you have a bad dream last night? Come on, wake up. We have to win this race."

Sekhem shoved a baton into Jon's hand. Jon took it and ran.

The relay race was set to begin in a short while. Across the courtyard, three other teams were also practicing passing the baton. Jon's teammate was Sekhem, one of Baka's cousins. Two other cousins, Aha and Osir, made up a second team. The last two teams were composed of friends and more distant relatives.

Jon ran up to Sekhem, passing the baton to him.

"That's more like it," Sekhem said with a smile. "Keep running like that, and we'll beat them easily."

Two palace guards stood at each of the four sides of the large courtyard. Several people, friends and family of the contestants, stood near the outer edges of the courtyard, excitedly waiting for the race to begin. Some of the spectators were cheering loudly, and placing bets on their favored teams.

The practice session ended, and the contestants approached the starting line. Out of the corner of his eye, Jon saw someone standing in the shadows, not far from one of the guards. The person came out of the shadows momentarily and appeared to say something to the guard. Then he darted back into the shadows, where a woman stood waiting. He spoke quickly to the woman, and they both disappeared into the palace. Jon turned to look, but he was not in time: he was unable to see either the man's or the woman's face. However, they probably weren't people he would have recognized anyway.

The four teams lined up. The race was about to begin. Sekhem held the baton, looking confident.

One of the palace guards called out, "Ready? On my signal."

Jon felt as if everyone's eyes were on him. He looked around nervously. Where was Neb? Probably invisible, Jon supposed. He hoped Neb was nearby. He also hoped he would run well and not disgrace Baka by losing the race.

The guard gave the signal, and the boys began to run. Sekhem quickly took the lead. He came alongside Jon and passed the baton smoothly. Jon picked up speed. He was tempted to look back, to see where the other runners were, but he knew that would just slow him down. He kept his eyes forward and continued running.

He circled around and passed the baton again to Sekhem, as he was supposed to do. Sekhem circled and passed the baton back to Jon. It was a long race, and Jon was getting tired, but he couldn't stop now. He was in the lead, and the finish line was not much farther.

Jon was vaguely aware of the other people in the courtyard near the finish line. He heard them shouting and cheering as he approached. He tried not to pay attention to them but to concentrate on his running. He almost didn't notice the dark shape that flew at him from above.

One of the palace guards gave a loud shout and ran forward, his arm waving wildly above his head. Another guard dropped to one knee, a bow in his hands, and quickly nocked an arrow to his bowstring.

Just in time, Jon saw the long, spread wings. The dark bird had its talons outstretched, ready to claw at Jon's face. The sharp beak opened menacingly. Jon quickly ducked, and the falcon barely missed him. Jon felt the wind from the fluttering wings as the bird wheeled around. He threw himself on the ground, but the bird had already flown away. He began to rise, and in the distance he saw the falcon circling, preparing to return for a second attempt.

As the bird approached again, the guard with the bow and arrow took aim, but his hands were shaking, and a look of terror was on his face. He kept his sight trained on the bird, but he did not release the arrow.

"Shoot!" yelled Sekhem at the guard. "Shoot. The falcon is approaching fast."

But the guard's hands shook even harder. "It is Horus," he said. "I must not shoot the god."

Sekhem pointed to the approaching falcon. "By all the gods!" He shouted at the guard. "Shoot, or you will have to answer to me. The next king is none other than the falcon-headed god on earth!"

The guard released his arrow. Jon watched as the arrow sped through the air towards the swooping falcon. The arrow missed, but not by very much. The falcon swerved away, breaking off his attack and flying outward again.

The guard nocked another arrow to his bow as the bird gained height and speed. At the far end of the courtyard, another bowman appeared and nocked an arrow to his bow too, but the bird was now too far away.

All eyes were on the dark object in the distance, beginning to approach for another attack. Jon rose and started running. He didn't think he had sufficient time to reach the safety of the building before the bird reached him, but at least he would try.

From behind him, Jon heard a rushing wind, similar to the sound the falcon had made in its first attack. Only this sound was much louder, as of a bird much larger than a falcon, and more powerful. Jon again threw himself on the ground. He looked up. The air was shimmering directly above his head, and he thought he felt the presence of something right above him, but besides the shimmering there was nothing to be seen. Beyond the palace walls Jon saw the falcon with his wings outstretched, approaching rapidly, no longer just a distant speck.

Jon crawled forward a short distance and quickly scrambled to his feet. There was no time for him to get away. Both guards released their arrows, but both missed their target by a long shot. Jon drew the short sword that hung from his belt. There was nothing to do now but to try defending himself as best he could against the bird's attack.

The falcon swooped down, his talons again outstretched, ready to tear at Jon's face. Jon swung his sword at the falcon. He missed, but still the sword seemed to strike something solid. Suddenly the bird stopped in mid-air, caught in an invisible net. Around the bird, the air was shimmering.

"Do not swing again." Neb's voice hung in the air above Jon's head. Jon looked up but saw nothing. Neb was invisible.

"I caught the falcon in an invisible net," Neb continued. "This is a trained falcon, trained to hunt. When you are safely inside the palace, I will release the bird. No doubt, he will return to his master, and I will follow him. Then I will know who sent him to attack you."

Everybody was staring at Jon and at the falcon caught in the invisible net.

"The bird is magical," Jon heard one of the guards cry out.

Another guard answered, "Horus the falcon-god has caught his bird in a magic trap, because he didn't want Prince Baka to be harmed."

Jon sheathed his sword and walked quickly to the end of the courtyard. Sekhem went with him. Jon nodded to the other royal cousins as he entered the palace.

Nobody dared approach the falcon, believing the bird to be a messenger of the god Horus. Neb, still invisible, released the net, and the bird hopped on the ground, fluttering its wings. Its eyes seemed to search the courtyard, as though looking for its prey. Then the bird took off, flying high above the courtyard.

The falcon wheeled around and flew over the palace walls. Neb followed, only with difficulty maintaining his invisibility as he gained speed. Suddenly an arrow appeared, shot from somewhere beyond the palace walls. The falcon gave a piercing cry that echoed through the still summer air. Then it fell to the ground lifeless, the arrow through its chest.

CHAPTER 9

THE ENEMY

"What happened, Neb?" asked Jon. "I thought you would protect me with your magic." Jon paced nervously back and forth across Prince Baka's secret room in the depths of the palace.

"My magic did protect you, didn't it?"

"Yes, said Jon. "But not at first. What happened?"

Both Jon and Baka had their eyes fixed on Neb, waiting for his reply. Neb lowered his head, and a look of embarrassment seemed to flicker for a moment across the sphinx's face.

"The bird could not have hurt you, Jon. Despite the scare you had, you were well protected. But you are right about one thing: it did not occur to me that they would use a bird for their attack. My enemies truly are ingenious, and I must wonder therefore whether there are other possibilities that I have missed."

Baka said, "It seems now that the risk for Jon is greater than we had thought at first. There is the possibility that our enemy will invent some method of attack against which your magic spells will not protect him."

"It seems unlikely," said Neb. "I have thought about it long and hard. The spells that I have used should be enough."

"They should," said Baka. "But still, you do not know for sure."

"You are quite correct," said Neb. "I do not know for sure. And so, I think we should ask Jonathan again whether he wants to continue with our plan."

Jon took a deep breath, brushing off the dangers that he had just faced. He smiled and said, "Of course I do. As you said, it's not just a coincidence that I look like him. There must be some reason for it. I mean, this is something I was meant to do."

Neb smiled. "Alright, then, let us think together. Jon, when you were in the courtyard did you notice anything at all that may have been suspicious? It may be something small and insignificant, something that you hardly noticed at the time."

Jon paced the floor, thinking. Suddenly he stopped.

"Hey, wait a minute. I did see something — I almost forgot."

Jon told Neb about the woman hidden in the shadows just before the race, and then Jon remembered something else about her: "I couldn't see her face," he said, "but by the way she dressed, I'd say she was a queen. She even walked like one."

"If you are right," said Neb, "that would be strange indeed. The king's wives do not usually go to that part of the palace. I will have to watch the royal wives more closely."

Princess Meres-ankh was pacing furiously back and forth in the courtyard of the women's quarters. Except for the princess and her mother Hetep, and a eunuch standing guard at the far end of the courtyard, there was no one else in sight. Hetep sat calmly on a stone bench as the princess paced in front of her. Also listening closely, at a slight distance behind Hetep, was Neb, invisible.

"I will not marry him. I can't," said the princess, waving her hands above her. "Surely you should understand! You were married once to a *real* prince. My father would have been a great king. But now he's dead, and so my good-for-nothing uncle sits upon the throne of Egypt. How does it feel to be the wife of such a man? His *second* wife, at that!"

Hetep's cheeks flushed for a moment, but her face remained calm, and her tone of voice was even. "You will not be a second wife to Baka. You will be his principal wife, the Great Royal Wife when he is king."

Princess Meres-ankh stopped pacing and looked at her mother. "Why are you pretending not to understand me? You know perfectly well what I mean. Do you not hear your sisters and your brothers talking? The common people may worship my uncle Djedef-Ra as a great king, a god on earth, Horus in the flesh. But to our family he is only a pretender, a man who plays at being king but is not worthy of the title. And, in my opinion, Baka is no better. I will not marry him."

Hetep smoothed her skirt with both her hands. She smiled at her daughter and said, "My dear Meri, it is almost nine years now since your beloved father died. He would have been a great king, but that was not to be. He was the oldest of King Khufu's sons, and all his brothers looked up to him. When your father died, there was much rivalry and much bitterness among the royal sons, each struggling to obtain King Khufu's favor. But Khufu surprised them all and chose your uncle Djedef-Ra to be his heir. Many of his brothers were older, and many had made great names for themselves in the army or in public works. But your grandfather chose wisely, ignoring age, ignoring empty titles and meaningless accomplishments. Instead, King Khufu chose from all his sons the one who had most wisdom and most skill in leading people. That son was Djedef-Ra."

Princess Meres-ankh began to speak, but her mother silenced her with an imperious wave of her hand.

"Do not believe the lies you hear about your uncle Djedef-Ra. They are merely tales and accusations invented by a group of jealous brothers, because Djedef-Ra is king and they are not. But you, my daughter, must consider what is best for you, and what will benefit your future most. Prince Baka will be king someday, and you will be his wife."

The princess began to pace again. "Are you finished talking?" she asked. Her mother nodded.

"Now listen to what I have to say. My answer still is no, and it will remain no. There is nothing you can say that will change my mind. I will not marry him."

Neb had heard enough. He was sure he would learn no further useful information if he stayed, and he was deeply troubled by what he had already heard. He floated over the courtyard wall and flew away. Below him lay the city of Memphis, the capital of Egypt, famed throughout the world for its magnificence and grandeur. But Neb hardly looked as he sped away, past the towers and the monuments and the city walls, outward towards the waiting desert. He flew above the great pyramid of Khufu, and the sun's rays caught his eye as they reflected off the pyramid's polished stones. He looked down and saw the many priests and visitors who bustled about the pyramid, worshiping at Khufu's temple or gazing upwards at the pyramid itself.

Neb thought about the future, about the millions of visitors and tourists who would come to see this sight during the centuries and millennia yet to come. He thought of the two great pyramids that later kings would build nearby to Khufu's. He imagined history unfolding before his eyes, and he thought of his own destiny, both past and future.

At length, Neb descended, far from the city, far from the pyramid and the temples. There was nothing in sight but sand and sun and sky. He was in the desert, where a person could feel the power of the gods reaching out, filling the human soul with insight and with wisdom. Here he could think and sort out in his mind what he had seen and heard.

Over the many centuries, Neb's remembrance of palace life had become blurred. But Princess Meres-ankh's argument with her mother had jolted Neb's memory. All the memories of palace plots and intrigues flooded his mind: the bitter jealousies among the nobles and the king's officials, the intense rivalry among the royal sons, the bribes and lies that were the daily tools of people seeking to advance themselves. But what stood out most of all in Neb's mind was the plotting and the power struggles among the royal women.

Could Princess Meres-ankh be the one behind the murders? She was still young, but the intensity of her feelings against Baka made her a suspect. Neb could not dismiss the possibility.

Hetep, too, was a suspect. After all, she once had been married to the royal heir, and now she was only the king's second wife. But Hetep had no sons, and her daughter Meres-ankh would be the queen someday, if she married Baka. What, then, would Hetep have to gain by murdering the king's heirs? Neb thought of several potential motives but finally dismissed them all as being too far-fetched.

Until today, Neb had thought the most likely person behind the murders would be one of the king's brothers. Certainly they had strong motives, and perhaps one or more than one of the brothers was involved in some way. But Neb was now convinced that the mastermind behind it all was someone else.

Here, in the stillness of the desert air, Neb could feel the power of the god who ruled this barren land: Set, the god of disorder, deserts, storms, and war. Neb hesitated momentarily, as he always did whenever he encountered Set. Set was surely among the greatest of the gods, but any close encounter with this god was filled with danger. For Set's power could throw confusion into the hearts of men, leading them astray, leading them to evil. Set's power was the source of evil in the world, but Set himself was neither good nor evil. Set was the force behind the turbulence of nature, the force behind the turbulence of man's spirit, and it was Set who held the key to the information that Neb sought. Yielding himself to the awesome forces of the desert, Neb opened his mind and soul, allowing his own powers to join with Set's.

"O mighty Set. Come to me, great god, you who knows the hearts of men. I seek your help, as I did so many times before, when I was still a man of flesh and blood. Great god, let your spirit enter into me, that I may see inside the heart of my true enemy."

For several moments, Neb's mind reached out in vain. And then, suddenly, he felt a distant presence, and he knew that he had found the one for whom he searched. He could not see his enemy's face or form, but through Set's vision he had glimpsed the spirit of his enemy. It was a woman's spirit.

Neb closed his eyes, struggling to focus his powers, to hold the woman's spirit in his mental grasp. But fast as lightning, she slipped away from him. Her spirit danced before him, taunting him to catch her. But every time he tried, she slipped away again.

Still he could not see her face, but he felt her smile. He heard her laugh. She was mocking him.

He tried harder. His mental powers probed in all directions like the tentacles of an octopus, reaching, searching, seeking to penetrate into the woman's soul, to see into her inner self, to see her face. Again he heard and felt her mocking laughter growing louder, ever louder, echoing in his ears.

Something stung at Neb's soul. Reaching out again with his magic powers, Neb felt the presence of another soul, filled with venom, lurking in the shadows of the woman's laughter. The laughter stopped, and the other soul made a sudden grasp for Neb. But Neb had felt the other's presence just in time.

Neb's mind withdrew quickly from the woman, but the other followed, pursuing the traces of Neb's retreating spirit into the desert. Neb felt the power of the other's soul; he felt the hatred and the jealousy directed toward him. He had no doubt that his pursuer was the sorcerer who had imprisoned him within the sphinx.

Neb opened his eyes. The sand was swirling all around him, rising higher and higher, swept upwards by the wind. He felt the sorcerer's powers groping at the air, trying to discover his location. Neb made himself invisible and moved backwards, away from the swirling sand, away from the sorcerer's grasp. But as he did so, the earth beneath him shook, and gradually a gaping hole opened in the ground before him.

From the hole in the ground a giant snake emerged, a monster that grew in size until it towered over Neb. It coiled itself up, rearing its head to strike, a king cobra with its golden hood majestically flaring outwards as its tongue probed the desert air, searching for Neb. It was clear this was no mortal snake, but a magic beast whose bite was death, even for a sphinx.

Still invisible, Neb backed away from the snake. But the serpent seemed to feel Neb's presence and lunged at Neb just as the sphinx launched himself into the air, narrowly escaping the cobra's deadly fangs.

Again and again the cobra struck, each time getting closer. Neb was tiring rapidly. The serpent's golden hood brushed against the sphinx's shoulder; and as Neb dodged the snake's attack, he felt the monster's evil breath upon his neck.

Neb's neck began to tingle where the serpent's breath had touched him. Quickly he felt the cobra's poisonous breath begin to overcome him. His mind began to blur, almost as though he had been drugged. As the snake attacked again, Neb stumbled, slipping backwards down a sand dune, and somehow barely managing to escape the cobra's deadly thrust.

He tried to fly away but found he could not do so. Again, as on the day of his murder, Neb felt the power of his enemy surrounding him, blocking his ability to summon magic to defend himself. He felt his magic powers fading quickly and knew the snake could now begin to see the outlines of his form. The cobra's head reared up again, preparing to attack one final time. Its cold eyes stared at Neb.

Neb tried to move away but could not. He was paralyzed, fixed in place by the serpent's gaze. He was now completely visible, defenseless, waiting for the snake to strike, expecting death.

The snake continued staring at its helpless prey. The great mouth opened, showing the cobra's fangs. A drop of venom trickled out and fell upon the desert sand, steaming as it hit the ground.

Neb knew he had to act immediately. When he had been a man of flesh and blood, his magic had not been strong enough to fight his enemy in the Anubis mask; and in the weeks since Neb's assassination, his enemy's power appeared to have increased still more. But now Neb also had the power of the sphinx at his command, and there was still one dreaded power deep within the sphinx's inner being that Neb had never used before. Momentarily he hesitated, fearing that even he would not be able to control the force that he unleashed. And yet, he had no other choice. With his last strength he summoned the sphinx's inner power, the power of the sphinx's *ankh* — its force of Life:

"Sphinx, you who hold me in your stony prison: I call upon your *ankh*. I know you are more powerful than I. I know I cannot control your fury. But merge your soul with mine this one time, and save me from my enemy."

He breathed in deeply as he felt a surge of savage power flowing through him, tearing at his human spirit. It was as though one half of him were making war upon the other half. Lion and man fought within his mind, each seeking to gain control, fighting for the prize of his immortal soul. He thought that he was going mad. He reared up on his hind legs, clawing at the air. Slowly, gradually, he felt his human mind regain control. He lowered himself to the ground again.

The sphinx's flowing mane shimmered in the desert air. His stony features came alive, his color changed from grayish-white to golden yellow, his body grew in size, and his face transformed into a lion's face, a lion more ferocious than any other lion that had ever walked the earth before. And yet, inside that lion's body, he still was mostly human. He was a living, breathing sphinx: part man, part beast.

The snake still stared at him, but the serpent's gaze no longer paralyzed him as it had done before. He shook his head, and the movement of his golden mane sent ripples through the desert air.

He looked into the serpent's eyes. Was it fear that he saw there? He raised his head and roared a long and mighty roar. The ground trembled before him. The cobra, frozen in place by the lion's roar, flared its hood but did not strike. The lion roared again, still louder and longer than before. And as he roared, the desert wind began to blow, sweeping up the sand that lay between the snake and Neb. The cobra, battered by the swirling sand, tried to uncoil its body and escape, but it was too late for that. A funnel of sand surrounded the great serpent and held him tightly in its grip. The snake squirmed and struggled to get free, but the whirling sand tightened its grip still more and pulled the serpent downward towards the desert floor. Then the wind retreated, while sand and snake together sank into the ground.

Neb circled the spot where the snake had been, pawing at the ground, making sure the snake was really gone. Then he let go of the sphinx's inner power, transforming himself again into the gray-white sphinx that he had been before his battle with the snake.

He sat down on the sand, exhausted. He needed to rest now, to regain his strength, but this was not the place to rest. He feared his enemy would return soon. He rose and started running.

The wind blew across the desert floor, shifting the sand around, making a whispering sound. The whispering grew louder. Neb stopped running and pricked up his ears, listening.

The wind stopped blowing, and a deep, whispering voice echoed out of the ground.

"Neb!" the voice called out.

Neb recognized the voice immediately: it was the jackal's voice.

"Neb, I see you have returned. I know your power, but you do not know mine. Enjoy your victory, vizier. It will not last. We shall meet again."

CHAPTER 10

TWO GOLD COINS

Neb flew deeper into the desert. The battle with the serpent had weakened him, and flying now was difficult. He landed on the desert floor. He looked around in all directions; he sniffed the desert air. When he was convinced that he was safe, he found a spot to rest.

After about an hour, Neb began to feel his strength returning. He tested his ability to make himself invisible. It took more effort than usual, and he was not sure how long he would be able to remain invisible, but he also knew he could not afford the luxury of waiting for his powers to return completely. Now he knew for sure that his assassin had not acted alone and that the person directing the murderer had been one of the royal women: perhaps one of King Djedef-Ra's wives or concubines, or more likely an aunt or sister of the king. Certainly there were many suspects, since even now, after eight years of rule, there still were many in the royal family who hated Djedef-Ra and still considered him unworthy to be king. Neb decided he must try to discover the woman's identity immediately. Now was the best time, since his enemies would not expect him so soon after his narrow escape from death.

Returning to the city, Neb made himself invisible. He floated above the women's quarters, watching the royal women come and go. The women's courtyard was full of activity. Several of the royal women were there, some accompanied by female slaves or eunuchs. Some of the women strolled along the garden paths, while others were taking shade beneath the palm trees that lined the courtyard paths.

Princess Nefer ran into the courtyard laughing and shouting merrily, accompanied by two female slaves, a eunuch, and a friend her own age. Nefer was Prince Baka's little sister, the daughter of King Djedef-Ra and Queen Tenka, the King's Principal Wife. Nefer's name meant "beautiful," and indeed she was.

Neb watched Nefer for a few minutes, fascinated by her lively personality and her graceful movements. He watched her throw a ball to her friend. He watched her run and catch the ball again. Even in her smallest movements, Neb could sense the power of her personality. *What a queen this girl will make someday!* he thought. But at present she was only nine years old and a most unlikely suspect.

After about an hour, Hetep entered the courtyard briefly and disappeared again. Neb supposed she had gone to her own chambers, since she did not emerge for perhaps an hour more. Finally she re-appeared, accompanied by a female slave.

Neb had been invisible for a long time, and he felt himself tiring. In the bustle of the women's courtyard, he hesitated to approach too closely. He feared that someone might bump into him, and, startled, he could briefly lose his invisibility. He approached as closely as he dared.

Hetep went over to one of the king's sisters and spoke to her. Soon they were joined by one of Hetep's sisters. Neb tried to listen to their conversation, but he was not close enough to hear. Only isolated words could he distinguish. However, none of the women was acting in a suspicious manner.

As the sun set, Neb left the courtyard, disappointed that he had not been able to discover any clues. Slowly he circled the women's quarters, wheeling about, preparing to return to the palace and to Baka's secret room. Suddenly, out of the corner of his eye, he saw a shadow streak across a nearby alley beyond the palace walls. He looked but saw nobody there. Slowly he descended, being careful not to move too fast and lose invisibility.

Neb waited, watching in the darkening twilight, but in the alley there was nothing. He began to doubt what he had seen. Nevertheless, he decided to wait and watch until it became completely dark. Many minutes passed. Slowly, a rear gate of the women's quarters opened, and a woman stepped out into the street. Neb tried to see her face, but she wore a veil, and it was nearly dark now. Neb could not identify her. Was she a noblewoman or a slave? He could not even be sure of that.

The woman turned her head first left, then right, her eyes scanning the street as she pulled the veil more tightly over her face. Quickly the woman crossed the street and darted towards the alley. A man appeared from between the buildings, and the woman spoke to him briefly, while handing him a small package. The man nodded and said something to her. It was nearly dark now, and Neb hovered closer, hoping to see more clearly and to overhear their words.

The woman's face was still hidden behind her veil, but Neb now saw the man's face clearly. It was a rough, weather-beaten face, bearing the effects of long exposure to the sun and wind, and punctuated by the marks of many brawls and street fights. The nose was flat and bent slightly to the right, and a deep scar ran from the man's left ear to the angle of his mouth. Neb knew he had never seen this man before.

The man clutched the package with one hand pressed closely against his chest. He held out his other hand, and the woman put two gold coins into it.

Neb tried to get still closer, knowing that this might be the last chance he had to find out the woman's identity. He was now within earshot.

"You will get the rest of the money when the entire business is concluded," the woman said.

A dog ran into the alley and stopped abruptly beneath the spot where Neb was hovering. The dog appeared clean and well groomed — probably a palace dog that somehow had gotten loose. The dog turned his head upwards, and the hairs on his back stood on end. Baring his teeth, he growled at the invisible Neb.

The woman, apparently shaken by the dog's sudden appearance and his bizarre behavior, said to the man, "Go quickly, and make sure you are not seen."

Without a word, the man nodded again and disappeared between the buildings. The woman looked around in all directions and retreated from the alley. Her face still veiled, she crossed the street and entered by the rear gate into the women's quarters. She walked with a confident stride, her head held high. It was the walk of royalty.

CHAPTER 11

THE DREAM

For the next three days, Jon saw very little of Neb. Invisible, the sphinx floated above the streets near the palace walls or near the women's quarters, alert to who was entering or leaving, hoping to recognize the woman he had seen at twilight in the alley, or at least to find a clue to her identity. Neb followed people out the gate and through the winding streets of Memphis, watching their every move and listening to their conversations when he could. At the end of each day, Neb, Baka, and Jon met in Baka's hidden room below the palace to discuss their findings. But after three whole days of searching in this way, they seemed no closer to discovering the identity of either the assassin who had murdered Neb or the royal woman who commanded him.

At their evening meetings, Baka seemed to be getting restless. He made it clear he wanted to play a more active role in the search. He was gradually recovering from his wounds, but Neb reminded him that it would be at least a few more days before he would be able to get out of bed and walk. He could not be seen in public yet. Jon would have to play Prince Baka for a while longer.

As Jon prepared to go to bed, he felt discouraged and very troubled. He had been counting on the assassin making some mistake and giving himself away. But so far, the assassin had made no mistakes. He was just too smart. Could it be that the assassin also had some magic power about which Neb had no knowledge? Could the assassin's magic be more powerful than Neb's? And, most troubling of all, if the assassin conquered Neb, how would Jon be able to return to his own time? There was a very real possibility that Jon could be stranded in ancient Egypt. He tried to put the thought out of his mind.

Jon lay in bed, trying to fall asleep, but sleep would not come to him. Every time he put one fear to rest, another doubt entered his mind. Again he tried to think of a way to unmask Neb's assassin. His thoughts drifted back to the falcon's attack. If only the bird had not been killed! If only Neb had been able to follow the falcon to its master! But the assassin had been too fast.

There can't be many people who could hit a falcon with an arrow at such a distance, Jon thought. The man who had shot the arrow must be an unbelievably good marksman. Maybe the way to find the assassin was to find out who was known for his skill with bow and arrow.

After a long time, Jon finally fell asleep. But he did not sleep well. He kept tossing about, sometimes groaning in his sleep. Even while asleep, his waking thoughts kept troubling him.

In a dream, Jon saw himself again in the palace courtyard with Baka's cousins. Just as they had done three days before, they were running a relay race. And once again, just like three days before, in Jon's dream a falcon swooped down at him from the clear blue sky. Just as he had done in real life, Jon now ducked and threw himself on the courtyard floor. The bird flew past him, crying out a challenge as it wheeled around, returning to attack again.

Again the falcon flew at him, his sharp beak open and his strong talons ready to seize Jon in their iron grip. Again Jon tried to duck, but this time, in his dream, the bird caught him by the neck and squeezed. Vaguely, Jon thought, *That's not how it happened. The bird never grabbed me.* But that thought failed to change his dream. Jon gasped and struggled with the bird; and yet, the falcon held on tightly and would not let go. The bird squeezed harder. Jon coughed and gagged. He tried to hit the falcon, to make the bird release its grip. Feathers flew. The falcon flapped its wings and let out a shrill cry. But still the talons held Jon's neck as firmly as before.

Jon woke up. A large man was bending over him, his hands around Jon's neck. Jon tried to scream but couldn't. He felt the pressure of the man's strong hands and wondered that he was able to breathe at all. But soon he realized that Neb's magic spell protected him, or else he would be dead already. Nevertheless, he couldn't count on Neb's magic spells. As soon as the man realized that strangling Jon would not work, he would surely try some other method. Neb had overlooked something before, so how could Jon be sure there wouldn't now be some way to penetrate the sphinx's protective spell? Jon felt he had to act fast, before the man tried a different tactic.

He struggled to get free, but the man was too strong for him. He tried to punch the man, first in the stomach and then in the face. But the man just laughed and dug his knee into Jon's belly.

With difficulty, Jon succeeded in raising his right shoulder. Then, with all his strength, he drove his right knee into the man's groin.

The man shouted out in pain. His grip on Jon's throat momentarily relaxed, and Jon seized his advantage. The man's hands were sweating, making them slippery. Jon twisted around quickly and succeeded in escaping from the large man's hold. Jon jumped off the bed and began to run towards the door, shouting.

The door opened, and two guards rushed in, their swords drawn. The guards immediately ran to the bed. They took hold of the man and raised him to his knees. The man didn't struggle. One of the guards held his sword to the man's throat.

"Speak, dog! Who are you?" the guard with the sword shouted.

But the man did not answer. He had failed to kill the prince, but he had made sure no one could question him. He was already dead, killed by his own hand with a dagger in his chest.

"He's dead," said the guard, as he released his lifeless prisoner.

Jon stood near the open door, still shaking from his brush with death. His nerves were on edge. From down the corridor he thought he heard a faint sound of footsteps.

Jon pointed out the door to his right. "Someone's out there," he said, his voice cracking.

The guards ran to the door. One of the guards ran down the corridor in the direction Jon had pointed. Shortly, he returned.

"Nobody was there, Your Highness" the guard said.

"Thank you," said Jon, wanting desperately to believe the guard. He wanted to believe that he had just imagined hearing footsteps in the corridor. But he could not convince himself of that, because at the instant that the guard had started running down the corridor, from the same direction Jon had heard another sound: the shutting of a door.

CHAPTER 12

LORD OF THE TWO LANDS

Djedef-Ra, King of Upper and Lower Egypt, Lord of the Two Lands, sat on his throne, his face angry. The throne room was filled with people, but no one spoke.

One by one, more people arrived. As each person entered, he went directly to his place, without even nodding to any of his friends. All eyes were on the king, waiting for him to speak.

Outside, now and then an owl hooted. It was still dark out, about an hour before dawn. Dogs barked as soldiers rushed through the streets holding torches in their hands. While most of the city slept, the soldiers knocked on doors of nobles and of high officials in the government, bringing them to the palace at the king's command.

At the entrance to the throne room and all along the walls, soldiers of the palace guard stood stiffly at attention, each holding a spear in one hand, a shield in the other. Their expressions were blank, hardly even blinking, but constantly alert, ready to spring into immediate action.

As each person entered the throne room, a guard directed him to his assigned section. In the first section were the royal women: wives and daughters, aunts and sisters of the king. Hetep was there, and Meres-ankh, seated next to Tenka the Great Royal Wife, and her daughter Nefer. Next to them was the King's Mother, Maat. And sitting beside her were Senna and Wepet, two of the king's stepmothers, Khufu's wives. When King Khufu lived, his wives had competed jealously for his attention and for power. And even now, eight years after Khufu's death, the jealous competition among his wives had not abated. If anything, it had grown still more intense. Senna and Wepet whispered to each other, frequently exchanging glances. They ignored Maat and did not even greet her when she entered. Maat appeared to be quite used to their behavior, and she ignored them too.

The king's male relatives sat in the next section. There were the king's half-brothers Minkhaf and Hur, and next to them sat Baka's cousin Sekhem. There were also many other cousins, brothers, and uncles of the king.

The third section was for the nobles. The fourth section was for the commanders of the army and of the palace guard. In the last section, the many government officials stood.

The king's half-brother Khaf-Ra entered, and a guard directed him. But on his way to his seat, Khaf-Ra stopped at the section of the royal women and gave his mother Senna a kiss on her cheek. Only then did he go to his assigned seat next to Hur, nodding to Hur and Minkhaf as he sat down.

King Djedef-Ra looked to his right and to his left, his gaze falling on each of his guests in turn. The king was not a large man, but his eyes were bright as fire. On his head he wore the double crown of Egypt: the tall, pointed white crown of Upper

Egypt mounted atop the flat red crown of Lower Egypt. Truly, as everybody knew, the king was a god himself: he was Horus the falcon-headed god, come down to earth in human form. It was said that Horus himself perched on the king's right shoulder, guiding him, giving him the power to see beyond what ordinary men could see. And each of the assembled guests felt the king's eyes burning into him, seeming to penetrate into the soul, examining the soul to see if it was pure.

A side door opened. Jon entered, dressed as Baka. A guard walked on either side of him. He went quickly to the throne and stood next to the king. King Djedef-Ra did not look at Jon, but he took Jon's hand in his own and held it tightly. In his other hand, the king held the *ankh*, symbol of life.

The king began to speak: "As many of you know by now, tonight there was an attempt against Prince Baka's life. Thanks to Horus's protection, the prince is safe, and the would-be murderer is dead. But the act that was committed, the attempt to kill the heir to Egypt's throne, is a terrible offence, an unforgivable sin against the king, against the land of Egypt, against the gods themselves."

Djedef-Ra paused, watching the effect of his words on the audience. There were some who looked surprised, but most appeared already to have known about the attempted assassination, probably informed of the news on their way into the palace.

The king's voice rose. "This was the second attack against the prince in the last few days. It was not the act of some crazed person attempting to commit a senseless murder. Nor was the motive merely jealousy or hatred against my son. Yes, jealousy and hatred were involved, indeed; but there was more. Much more. Someone is attempting to upset the equilibrium of Egypt, to disrupt the delicate balance in the land. Someone is seeking power for himself. And who is this someone? It is one who is powerful already, but is not satisfied with what he has. I have reason to believe that it is one among you who is plotting to assassinate my son."

People looked at each other. A murmur rose up among the guests. King Djedef-Ra's eyes scanned the audience, noting the expressions on the faces of his subjects. If there had been little surprise before at the announcement that someone had attempted to assassinate the prince, the king's suspicion that a person here among them in the throne room had planned the deed seemed to disturb almost everyone. In fact, the king's suspicions should not have been a surprise to anyone: the people assembled here in the throne room were the obvious suspects. But what was so disturbing was hearing the king speak his suspicions aloud in public, having the god-king, speaking with the authority of Horus, address them directly and cast his gaze upon them as he spoke his accusation. Certainly the nobles, the commanders of the army, and the commander of the palace guard all had looks of hurt or disbelief. Only the guards who stood at the doors and along the walls seemed almost unaffected by the king's words. They continued standing stiffly at attention, their faces blank. Only the king himself noticed the blinking of the guards' eyes, the increased tension in the muscles of their arms, the tightening of their grips as they held their spears.

The royal wives and daughters shook their heads and looked suspiciously at everyone around. And many of King Djedef-Ra's brothers and sisters shook their heads in disbelief and whispered to each other when they thought the king did not see them. But Djedef-Ra did see, and he took careful note of how each one reacted.

The king let go of Jon's hand and raised his own hand for silence. Immediately the murmuring stopped, and the king continued speaking:

"You who are assembled in this room are the leading people in the land of Egypt. You are the chosen, beloved of the gods. You are the most privileged in the land. To some of you the gods have given wealth; to some the gods have given power and authority. You are the king's advisors, and the fate of Egypt lies within your hands. You have achieved high office, some of you by birth and some because of your hard work and inborn talents. The common folk look up to you, and your king has put his trust in you. Yet one among you has abused that trust: one among you is a traitor!"

The king's eyes flicked back and forth across the room, and his voice rose in anger. "To the traitor I have this to say: do not think you will escape from me. I swear to you by Horus and by all the gods of Egypt that I will find you out. And when I do, I swear to you, your punishment will be terrible. Therefore I advise you to flee the country now. Run away, before you are discovered and condemned to painful death. Leave the land of Egypt, never to return, you and all who joined you in your traitorous acts."

CHAPTER 13

THE CROCODILE

Sobek closed the door, nodded to the two guards standing by, and walked quickly down the winding hallway. As he walked, his hand went to the hilt of the sword hanging at his hip. For a moment, he wrapped his fingers around the hilt and then quickly released it. It was unlikely he would need to use the sword today, but, as always, it was reassuring to feel the weapon at his side.

All morning, since before sunrise, Sobek had gone from room to room, talking in private to each of the king's aunts and uncles, sisters, wives, and brothers, and to each of the most important nobles in the kingdom. By the king's order, all suspects were to remain confined to the palace or to the women's quarters until Sobek, Captain of the Palace Guard, had personally questioned them. Members of the royal family who lived in the palace or in the women's quarters were to be questioned in their own chambers. A scribe went with Sobek as he questioned each suspect, recording the interrogation for the public record. It was late morning already, and Sobek had gone through less than half the list of suspects. It would be a long, hard day for the Captain of the Palace Guard.

Sobek, named for a crocodile-headed god, had always been proud of his awesome name and tried to conduct his life as though he were the living spirit of the god whose name he bore. All men feared him, except perhaps the king, and that was as it should be, Sobek told himself.

Sobek had just finished questioning Baka's cousin Sekhem. A less likely suspect would be hard to find. Sekhem was always hanging around Baka, laughing, joking, talking seriously, or playing games. More than a cousin, Sekhem was Baka's greatest friend, and so they had been since early childhood. Of course, there was the possibility that Sekhem was just acting, pretending to be the prince's friend while secretly plotting against him; but Sobek knew that was not the case. Moreover, even if there were evidence incriminating Sekhem, Sobek knew it would be difficult to convince the king of Sekhem's guilt. Nevertheless, it had been necessary to question Sekhem just like all the other suspects.

Sobek had done his duty: he had questioned Sekhem thoroughly, in fact much more so than was necessary. But it had been fun, and Sobek smiled now as he thought about it. Sobek enjoyed playing the game of cat-and-mouse with his suspects; he enjoyed asking people probing questions; and he enjoyed putting people on the defensive and watching them squirm. He was proud of the thoroughness with which he interrogated suspects. Never let it be said that Sobek, Captain of the Palace Guard, had failed to put his full effort into the performance of his duty!

Sobek paused in front of a door. He waited until the two guards who he knew were following him came into view. Then he knocked, identified himself, and let himself in.

The room was large and beautifully decorated, as was fitting for a brother of the king. The royal brothers did not live within the palace but had homes in other parts of the city or elsewhere in the land of Egypt. This was a guest room used for the royal brothers when they visited the palace. There were several large, ornamented chairs scattered about the room. Sobek chose one of them and sat down facing his next suspect: Hur, son of Khufu, and King Djedef-Ra's older half-brother.

During the last years of Khufu's reign, Prince Hur had been vizier to Khufu. As vizier, Hur had earned the respect of all of Egypt. He was known throughout the Two Lands for his great wisdom, his devotion to the gods, and his knowledge of the magic arts. Many even thought he would make a great king. When Khufu died, Hur, along with his brother Minkhaf, had led the opposition against Prince Djedef-Ra. But Djedef-Ra had had his father Khufu's blessings and, despite all opposition, had been crowned king. Minkhaf, as leader of the opposition, had been banished from the capital. Hur had not been exiled from Memphis, but he had been dismissed as vizier and had been forced to agree to stay out of the public eye. He now lived in a home at the far end of the city. Hur had sworn allegiance to Djedef-Ra, but Sobek thought it likely that hatred still boiled in the depths of Hur's heart, just as Sobek had a special hatred for him even after all these years. Sobek looked forward to interrogating Hur.

The scribe took a seat at Sobek's side, put a writing board on his lap, and carefully spread a sheet of papyrus over the board. While the scribe was preparing his writing equipment, Sobek looked around the room, occasionally throwing sidelong glances at Hur. The scribe tested the tip of his reed pen with the pad of his index finger, dipped the pen into ink, and nodded at Sobek.

To the scribe, Sobek said, "Let the record show that we are interviewing Prince Hur, older half-brother of King Djedef-Ra, and former vizier during his father Kufu's reign."

Sobek abruptly turned his eyes to Hur. "Where were you last night?"

Sobek's sharp gaze tore at Hur's face. Sobek's voice pierced Hur's heart and made him tremble. With satisfaction, the Captain of the Palace Guard noted the beads of sweat on the suspect's forehead. Sobek did not think it was just the heat that made Hur sweat.

"Asleep. At home, in bed," Hur answered.

"And before that?"

"Also at home, entertaining guests."

"Do you have witnesses to vouch for you?"

"Yes, several. Huni, Iri, Kamose . . ."

"That's enough. At what time did you go to bed last night?"

"About two hours after nightfall."

"Did you fall asleep immediately?"

"No," said Hur.

"And is that unusual for you?"

"Yes, it is," Hur answered.

"What kept you awake, my lord? Was something troubling you perhaps?"

"Possibly," said the prince. "But it must have been important only for the moment, since I do not remember what it was."

"When did you first learn of the attack against Prince Baka?"

"As I said, I was asleep. I knew nothing of the attack until the king's messengers awoke me and summoned me to the palace."

"Where were you on the day Prince Baka was attacked by the falcon in the palace courtyard?"

Hur named an inn outside Memphis and again listed several witnesses. Sobek noticed that Hur was beginning to relax a bit, and Sobek knew exactly what the prince was thinking now: Sobek's questions were not as difficult as Hur had feared.

Sobek smiled. It was not a pleasant smile. "Your Highness, do you remember Neb, the king's vizier?"

The question seemed to take Hur by surprise. He hesitated just a moment before answering. "Of course I do," he said.

Sobek paused, observing Hur's growing fear. "As you know, Your Highness, Neb died several weeks ago under suspicious circumstances. Just today my men discovered evidence that may tie one of your servants to that crime. Where were you on the day that Neb was poisoned?"

Hur's face turned pale. "Which of my servants do you mean?"

As Sobek knew, there was no evidence against any of Hur's servants, but Hur had no way of knowing that. Let Hur think there was such evidence. Fear often causes a man to make mistakes. Sobek smiled again. "I am not allowed to say. Now please answer my question: where were you when Neb was murdered, and on the previous day?"

Hur sat up straight. He looked Sobek in the eye and said, "That was a long time ago. Several weeks. I will have to go home and check my records. Then I will give you my answer."

"Records can be altered when it suits the need. With all due respect, my lord, you are under suspicion. I will send a palace guardsman to escort you, and a scribe also. They will assist you as you review your records."

Prince Hur rose from his seat and began to speak, but Sobek held his hand up.

Turning to the scribe, Sobek said, "Let the record state that when King Khufu died, Prince Hur joined his brother Minkhaf in opposition to Djedef-Ra's inauguration."

Prince Hur looked offended. "That is ancient history. It is not relevant."

Ignoring Prince Hur's outburst, Sobek continued: "Let the record also note that, for that offence Prince Hur was dismissed as the king's vizier, and Neb was appointed in his place. Thus, despite Prince Hur's oath of allegiance to his brother Djedef-Ra, Hur has a motive, and suspicion rests on him."

"This is preposterous!" Hur shouted.

His head still turned to the scribe, Sobek said calmly, "That will be all."

The scribe rolled up his papyrus sheet, and Sobek left the room while Hur waited for his escort to arrive. Everything was going very well, Sobek decided. Although there was still no evidence connecting Hur to the attack on Baka, if Sobek could link Hur to Neb's assassination, that would be a good beginning. Surely Hur had a motive to attack the royal family. Now it was just a matter of time, Sobek thought, and Hur would soon be caught.

CHAPTER 14

MEMORIES

The next day

J on awoke in Baka's chamber. The sun had already risen and was shining brightly through the window. Jon squinted and rubbed the sleep out of his eyes. Even after several days pretending to be Baka, Jon still felt strange lying in Baka's bed while the prince himself remained in the secret chamber below the palace. Jon looked around the room. Neb was in the corner, observing him.

"Did you sleep well, Your Highness?"

"Please don't call me that. It's not right. Hey, what are you doing here anyway?"

Neb smiled. "I entered through the window while you slept. But why should I not address you as 'Your Highness'? Even Baka's father calls you prince, although he knows quite well that you are merely one who looks like Baka. I see that you have changed since we arrived here not so long ago. When you first met Baka, you were so eager to take his place. Now you know how difficult it is to be a prince and how the honor that accompanies the title must be earned. But you have been courageous, and I think that you have earned the right to be a temporary prince."

Jon swung his feet over the side of the bed. "And where were you all of yesterday? I didn't see you anywhere. I was getting worried."

Neb twitched his ears. "I am truly sorry that my absence got you worried, Jonathan, but I had much to do."

Jon was about to say something, but Neb interrupted: "Do not be alarmed. I spun a magic link between my soul and yours. Even when I am far away, I still can sense your *ka* and know that all is well with you. My magic still protected you, even from the distance."

Jon looked doubtful. After a brief silence, the suggestion of a grin formed at the corners of his mouth. "OK, then. Where was I yesterday?" he challenged.

"You spent the day searching all the chambers along the corridor to the right of this chamber where we are right now. As for me, I returned to the tomb where my body was buried, to search for clues to the magic spell my enemy used."

"Did you find anything?"

Neb swished his tail. "There were new inscriptions on the walls. But they were only standard incantations, words to say when, after death, the soul will face Anubis, the eternal judge."

"Hey, isn't Anubis the god with the jackal's head?"

"That's right," said Neb.

"And in the museum, didn't you tell me that the guy who killed you wore a jackal mask?"

"That is correct. He wore a mask to hide his face, because he was probably someone whom I knew. But also, he chose to play

Anubis to let me know that he had judged my soul and condemned me to my fate."

"You spent all day there. You must have found something."

"There were many inscriptions, and I read them all. But nothing even hinted to the spell that my assassin used. I read all the inscriptions a second time, just to be sure I hadn't missed anything. But I found nothing even slightly useful. Then I went outside, and there it was: the sphinx in which my *ka* was trapped was standing guard outside my tomb."

"Wow! That must have been really weird — seeing yourself, I mean your sphinx self."

"Yes, it was indeed. It almost seems impossible that I could meet up with myself. I felt like a ghost, a future image of the real stone statue that I saw before me. I looked at the statue's face: it was my face engraved in stone, the image of the face I had when I was still a man of flesh and blood. I wondered whether I could talk to it, perhaps communicate with my *ka* just recently imprisoned deep within this stony sphinx. I tried, and tried again. I tried and failed. And then I thought about that day of terror many years ago. Through the centuries, often I had tried to recollect what happened in the first few days and weeks that I had spent inside the sphinx, without success. But yesterday, as I looked into the stony sphinx's eyes, the memories of that day returned to me, and I relived my long-forgotten past."

"That's amazing, Neb. What did you remember?"

"My *ka* had just been torn from my human body and had entered the sphinx at jackal-head's command. I felt my soul uniting with the sphinx's body. There was a feeling of great power within that statue, but it was a power far beyond me, and it would be at least a century before I could learn to control it. I looked for the first time through the sphinx's eyes and saw my assassin standing in the desert, in the blinding early morning light. He looked at the sphinx, appearing pleased. Then he turned his face away, and suddenly he vanished. I was left alone.

"The sun was overhead when he returned. I did not see him, but I heard him speak behind me to another man. I heard them lifting something heavy. I knew it was my poisoned body that they lifted, intending to bring it into Memphis in the night and leave it somewhere in the city to be found.

"I was left alone again, with only the desert sand and wind for company. I felt the spirit of Set moving through the vast emptiness before me. Lord of the desert, god of war, his warm breath blew upon me, stroking me. My assassin had sought to use Set's spirit. But Set himself is uncontrollable. His awesome power can be used at times, but only briefly and with his consent. Set, most terrible of gods, is unpredictable. Sometimes he lashes out with violence and destruction, whereas at other times his spirit fills men's hearts with understanding and with wisdom. Now he seemed to favor me again, and my soul drank his power, which I would someday learn to use. In later years, I would also learn to use the powers of many other gods and goddesses: Horus, Ra, Osiris, Isis, Hathor, Thoth, and Ptah. But that day I was in the desert, land of Set, and it was of his spirit that my soul drank thirstily.

"Weeks passed before my jackal-headed enemy returned again. This time he came with slaves and wagons. They put the sphinx in an ox-drawn cart, and slowly they brought me through the desert, to Memphis, to be placed before the entrance of my tomb."

"Wow! That's some story, Neb. And in all those years you never remembered any of it till yesterday?"

"That is correct."

"What did you do after the memories came back to you?"

"I flew out into the desert, looking for the place where I was killed. The great hall where the sorcerer with the jackal mask confronted me was undoubtedly a secret temple dedicated to the worship of Set. But the temple was built underground, its entrance hidden. I thought I knew the general location, and I prayed to Set to help me find the entrance. But Set did not answer me; I searched in vain."

"That's too bad," said Jon. "My luck wasn't any better than yours. Worse, actually. At least you found some lost memories. I found nothing."

"What were you looking for?"

Jon smiled and said: "Clues, just like you."

Jon told Neb about the door he heard closing after the attack that had awakened him from his sleep two nights ago.

"So you were trying to determine which door it was. But when you find the door, how will you know that it is indeed the door your heard that night?"

"I'm learning from you, Neb. Things don't just happen by chance. I'm not really sure what I'm looking for. But when I find the clue I'm looking for, I'll know it. It's there, somewhere down that hallway. I know it is. Tomorrow I'll search again."

CHAPTER 15

SEARCHING FOR CLUES

The following day

Sobek left Princess Meres-ankh's chamber and walked quickly down the corridor of the women's quarters, the scribe scurrying behind him struggling to keep up. Today was the second day of the interrogations, and it was already approaching noon. Sobek was determined to finish questioning all the suspects by noon tomorrow. His men were still working to gather some last bits of evidence, and Sobek expected they would finish tomorrow afternoon. By late tomorrow or early on the following day, he would be ready to make an arrest. The king was pressing him to make a quick arrest, but first Sobek had to make sure his case was strong and would convince a court of law. Furthermore, Sobek believed in planning for all eventualities; if the first suspect were acquitted, Sobek would have to be prepared to arrest a second suspect quickly. As he walked along the winding halls of the women's quarters to his next interrogation, Sobek reviewed in his mind the evidence against each of the suspects he questioned.

This morning he had re-interrogated three of the king's half-brothers: Khaf-Ra, Hur, and Minkhaf. Khaf-Ra, who was younger than most of the king's other siblings, had done nothing in particular to raise suspicion, and, unlike some of his other relatives, he was on good terms with the king. Nevertheless, Khaf-Ra's mother was Senna, and she had become King Khufu's principal wife after Khufu's first wife had died. That fact alone was enough to make Khaf-Ra a leading suspect.

As for Hur and Minkhaf, everybody knew about their rivalry with Djedef-Ra and about the bitterness that burned within their hearts. King Djedef-Ra may have pardoned them, but neither Djedef-Ra nor any of his subjects could forget how Hur and Minkhaf had once attempted to prevent their brother from inheriting their father's throne. Both of them were likely suspects, but Hur lived in Memphis and therefore had more opportunity than Minkhaf who lived in distant Waset. Moreover, Hur was the son of Khufu's first wife, and Hur had also been vizier to Khufu. And lastly, Sobek smiled as he thought of the evidence his men had found in searching Prince Hur's house while Sobek was interrogating him today. Sobek thought it likely that even now the prince was unaware that any evidence had been discovered in his home.

Of the royal women, neither the king's mother nor his principal wife seemed a likely suspect, although Sobek had made a point to question both of them a second time. As for Hetep, she was King Djedef-Ra's second wife, and Prince Baka was not her son. But Hetep did not seem a very likely suspect either, since her daughter Meres-ankh was to marry Baka soon, and Hetep had no sons herself.

Princess Meres-ankh had been uncooperative with Sobek's questions, and her antagonism had grown as the interrogation proceeded. Sobek might have interpreted her behavior as evidence of guilt, but Sobek knew that she was merely being stubborn as any normal teen-age princess might be. Perhaps, he thought, she was hiding other secrets unrelated to the royal murders and the attempts on Baka's life, but that would be an investigation for another time. Sobek knew that his investigation had to appear unbiased and objective. At present, he decided, there was nothing to suggest Meres-ankh's guilt. However, he was not aware of her refusal to marry Baka.

While Sobek interrogated the royal women and Baka still lay in bed in his secret chamber below the palace, Jon went from room to room in the main wing of the palace, searching for clues. Jon softly closed the door behind him. He had just searched a chamber four doors to the right of Baka's door. He had found nothing of value.

To Jon's left, two guards were coming towards him, talking and laughing loudly. It was daytime, but the corridors between the chambers had no windows, and the guards were carrying a torch to light their way. The flame of their torch flickered in the distance, casting dancing shadows on the wall. Even though Baka's chamber was nearby, normally he would have been attending to various royal duties at this time, and Jon thought it would look suspicious if he were seen here now. Jon pressed himself against the wall. His eyes darted to and fro, looking for a hiding place.

He heard the guards stop. They knocked on a door and waited. There was no reply.

Jon considered sneaking down the corridor away from the guards. They were still somewhat distant, but the corridor was straight, and he thought they might notice him if he moved. Or else, they might hear the echo of his footsteps on the stone floor.

Jon slid down close to the floor and crept a short distance, still pressed against the wall. He heard the guards begin to walk towards him again. He crawled forward a few more paces.

A third guard came up behind the other two. He was also carrying a torch. "Have you seen Sobek anywhere?" he asked.

"No. I think he is now in the women's quarters," one of the other two replied.

The third guard went back in the direction from which he had come. The two remaining guards watched him go. They waited until he was out of earshot before either of them spoke again.

"I'll bet Sobek's enjoying himself there in the women's quarters, searching all the women's rooms. I hope he stays there a long time. The less I see of him, the better."

"I agree with that! Ever see the way he questions suspects? He really is exactly like the god whose named he bears. Sobek the crocodile! I can just imagine him as a crocodile, with his mouth wide open, his sharp teeth beckoning, ready to rip a man to shreds." The guard spread his arms and opened his mouth, mimicking a lurking crocodile.

The first guard said, "You're right: his name sure fits his personality; but I really can't think of him as a god, not even a crocodile-headed god."

"Well, maybe not a god, but he's got powers anyway. Have you ever seen the look in his eyes when he is mad? That look could turn you to stone if he wanted it, and I mean that literally. He really could, you know."

There was a brief silence. Then both guards laughed loudly and started walking again towards Jon.

Jon crawled forward on his hands and knees, trying his best to be silent. A rough stone in the floor scraped his knee. He almost cried out in pain but stopped himself in time. He raised his knee a little and looked at it. It was bleeding.

While staying close against the right-hand wall, Jon scurried along the corridor, his head bent, his body crouched. The guards were still walking, approaching Jon. Ahead of him, a chamber door was partly open. A sliver of light from beyond the door illuminated the adjacent corridor. Jon didn't think he could cross the lightened area now without being seen. Quickly he slid into the chamber, leaving the door open behind him.

The room was large, with colorful paintings decorating each of the walls. Statues of animal-headed gods and goddesses lined the two walls to either side of the door. In the middle of the room there was a table covered with a brightly painted tablecloth upon which there were at least a dozen ceremonial objects that Jon could not identify. At the far end of the room there was a large, golden disk representing the sun-god Ra, supreme god of Egypt, protector of the king. The disk was placed at an angle to the window, so that the sun's rays reflected off the shiny metal surface. Just in front of the sun disk there was an altar, and on the altar there was incense burning. Jon ran to the altar and hid behind it, directly under the gleaming disk of Ra.

No sooner had Jon hidden himself than the door was thrown fully open, and the two guards walked in.

"See? There's nothing here," said one of the guards.

"I'm not so sure of that," said the other. "Let's look around."

"Are you crazy, Anu? This place is holy. We shouldn't even be in here. We could get into trouble. Let's go."

The guard named Anu drew his sword and looked under the table in the middle of the room. Then he moved to the right and started looking behind the statues. Jon held his breath and tried not to move.

"Come on, Anu. We can't stay here," the first guard said again.

"I tell you, I'm sure I saw somebody go into this chamber. Get over here, and help me search."

The first guard moved slowly to the left, searching behind the statues. He did not draw his sword.

As Anu approached from the right, Jon realized he could not stay where he was or he would soon be discovered. He slid along the far side of the altar away from Anu, while trying to keep his distance also from the guard on the left and hoping that guard would not see him. At least for the moment, there were statues between him and the guard.

Jon slid around to the front of the altar just as Anu was coming around the other side. Jon waited a for a few moments. When he figured that Anu was directly behind the altar, Jon quickly crept to the table in the center of the room. He slipped under the tablecloth and waited.

"There's no one here," said the first guard as he met up with Anu behind the altar.

Anu didn't answer, but both guards started to move slowly towards the middle of the room. Jon was sure that Anu had signaled to the other guard, and now they were coming towards him. It was likely that Anu would look under the table again.

Quickly, Jon rose, lifting the table. It wasn't heavy, and he threw it at the two guards. The ceremonial objects on the table came crashing down, scattering on the floor in front of the guards. As the table knocked the guards off balance, Jon ran towards the door and out into the corridor. As he left the chamber, Jon turned left and ran back in the direction from which he had come before. He heard the two guards running after him.

The guards paused to retrieve the torch that they had left in a sconce on the corridor wall. There was only one torch, and they would therefore have to stay together. Jon hoped they would pick the wrong direction.

"Which way did he go?"

"There's blood on the floor here. This way!"

Behind him, Jon heard the two guards running again. They were running in his direction. Jon ran, staying close to the wall.

"Stop!" one of the guards called out. "In the king's name, I order you to halt!"

Jon was getting out of breath, but he knew he couldn't stop. He continued to move along the wall until he came upon a spot where the wall curved outwards slightly, forming a small recess off the corridor. He slid into the recess and waited.

The two guards ran past. Jon pressed his body against the stone wall and rested his hand against the wall near the floor. To his surprise, his fingers touched a metal object wedged inside the rock. Down the corridor, he heard the two guards stop.

"We lost him."

"No, we didn't," the other guard said. "I think we passed him back there, hiding in the darkness." The guards started back in Jon's direction.

Jon knew he didn't have much time. He didn't think he could outrun the guards for long. Frantically, he pushed against the metal object in the rock and felt the wall push back a bit. He put his hand into the crack, and then his entire arm. He felt a metal bar. He pulled and felt a click, but nothing moved. He tried to pull harder, but the bar was stuck and would move no further.

The guards were approaching, and they were now only about twenty five paces from him. Jon wedged his shoulder against the wall and pushed with all his strength. The wall pushed back, revealing a black tunnel.

Jon looked behind him and saw a torch mounted on the wall of the corridor a short distance away. He wanted to go and take it, but he knew he would be seen. He plunged into the darkness of the tunnel.

He kept his left hand on the tunnel wall to guide him as he moved forward. He felt a rope and a wheel, apparently some kind of pulley. Quickly he pulled on the rope, and the wall behind him softly swiveled shut.

Jon was sure this was the door that he had heard squeaking shut after the almost-fatal attack in Baka's chamber: a hidden door into a secret passageway. But why did it not squeak now? He ran his hand over the wall. He felt the metal hinge on which the door had swiveled open. It was wet with oil. Someone had oiled it recently.

Beyond the wall, Jon heard the two guards talking:

"I could have sworn I saw him about here."

"Yeah, me too," said Anu. "I think he was hiding here in this recess in the wall, but now he's gone. He just vanished. What'll we tell Sobek?"

There was a slight hesitation before the other guard answered. "Some things are better left unsaid. Who says Sobek's got to know?"

The two guards walked away in silence, and Jon was left alone in the darkness of the tunnel.

CHAPTER 16

THE QUEEN

Jon's eyes soon began to adjust, and he realized it was not completely dark in the tunnel. A faint glow shone from the walls. It was rather eery, and not nearly enough to light the way, but it was better than total darkness.

Jon kept his left hand on the wall as he moved slowly forward, being careful not to trip and fall. He tried not to make any sound.

Jon inched his way through the near-darkness. Several times he thought he heard someone else's footsteps echoing through the tunnel. Each time, he stopped to listen, but each time the sound of footsteps quickly disappeared.

After about ten minutes, the tunnel came to a dead end. Jon put his hand on the far wall. Now that he knew what he was looking for, it was not difficult. He bent down and found a metal bar protruding from the wall. He was about to pull the bar when he heard voices.

Jon froze, listening. At first he thought the voices were coming from behind him in the tunnel. It took a few seconds before he realized that the sound was coming from beyond the wall. Through the stone wall the voices were muffled, and Jon was not able to distinguish words. But of one thing he was certain: they were women's voices.

Jon waited until it was quiet again. Slowly he pulled the metal bar back, and the tunnel wall opened just a crack. Jon peered through the crack. There was nobody in sight. Still, he hesitated to open the door further. What if someone was there after all? But he knew he had to come out of the tunnel eventually; and the longer he waited, the greater was the chance that someone would pass by and see the opening in the wall. Quickly, he pulled the bar back all the way, swinging the wall open. He stepped out of the darkness and closed the secret door.

Jon looked around, squinting in the light. He was in a hidden corner off the main corridor, and he was fairly sure that nobody had seen him emerge from the tunnel. A few steps away, in the main corridor, a group of women were walking by, talking to each other and laughing merrily. None of them looked his way.

He looked at the women's faces. Some of them appeared vaguely familiar, but he couldn't identify any of them. He thought back to yesterday morning when the king had addressed the people in the throne room. Jon supposed he should have remembered some of these women from there; but at the time, he had concentrated all his efforts on trying to look like a prince in front of all those people. Also, the king's speech in the throne room had occurred only a short while after the attack that had jolted Jon from sleep, and he probably had not been paying as close attention as he might have normally.

After several minutes, the way was clear, and Jon emerged from hiding. He darted down the corridor and found another hiding place before any other women passed. He had no idea where he was going, but he did know he was somewhere in the women's quarters.

The corridor opened into a garden. The ceiling was open to the sky, and sunlight filled the garden. Jon slunk around the edge of the garden, hiding behind bushes. Just as he entered another corridor, a door opened, and Jon hid in a corner behind a statue. He looked but saw nobody. He heard whispering through the open door. There were two voices, and one of them was a man's voice.

The door opened wider, and a man emerged, walking quickly down the corridor away from Jon. Jon tried his best but could not see the man's face before he disappeared around a corner.

The door closed. Jon stayed in his hiding place, hoping the woman would come out also. He waited for a long time.

When he was almost about to give up and leave, the door opened again, and a woman stepped out of the room. She looked in both directions before she slowly closed her door.

She walked towards Jon, but he was unable to see her face clearly. She passed Jon's hiding place. Walking to the end of the corridor, she stood still for a short while. Jon thought she was watching something or somebody in the garden.

She turned around and walked back again towards her chamber. Jon saw she wore a golden necklace. Her eyes were outlined in black, and her lips were painted red. Her dark hair hung over her shoulders, ornamented with fine gold chains. A sudden dread came over Jon. He had not seen her face, yet somehow Jon was sure he knew this woman, and not from yesterday's gathering in the throne room but from someplace else. As she approached, Jon craned his head to see her face.

Again she stopped and turned around, away from Jon. For about a minute she stood watching the garden beyond the corridor. Then she turned back in Jon's direction and continued walking towards her chamber.

The woman's face came into view. Jon gasped and almost jumped up out of his hiding place behind the statue. Now he recognized her. In his imagination, he felt her presence floating in the air above him, and in his mind he heard her voice.

"Go back!" said the woman's image in Jon's mind. "Do not listen to the sphinx. His way will lead to death. You have been warned."

The image faded from Jon's mind, and he looked again at the woman who was passing by him in the corridor. There was no doubt about it now: this woman was the queen whose spirit had threatened him at the museum.

CHAPTER 17

MUT

Jon nodded to the guard and entered Baka's secret room beneath the palace. He was eager to tell about what he had seen in the women's quarters. But as he entered the room, he found Neb and Baka in the middle of a heated conversation, and he knew immediately that his report would have to wait.

"If only I could have seen her face," Neb was saying.

Baka sat up in bed, his face red. He slammed his hand down on the bedside table. "You do not need to see her face! I know exactly who she was. She could only have been Hetep, my father's *other* wife. And I don't think there's any mystery about what she was doing either: she was paying an assassin to have me killed."

"You cannot know that for sure," Neb said. "In fact, I doubt it."

Baka began to rise, his muscles tense. "I know Hetep. She speaks well of me to others; but in her heart, I know she hates me. Do not believe a word of what she says. She is the one who wants me dead; she is the one who had my brothers killed; and she is the one who tried to have me killed three times already. We should send the Captain of the Guard to arrest her immediately. Guard! Come . . . ."

But Neb had apparently anticipated Baka, and as the prince began to raise his voice to call the guard, the sphinx lifted up his right front paw. A shimmering wall of air immediately materialized before the chamber door, reflecting Baka's voice to echo through the room.

"Wait, my prince," said Neb. "Do not be so hasty. First, whatever you may think, the evidence is not sufficient yet. Second, do not forget her accomplice, the man who killed my body and condemned my soul to live imprisoned in the sphinx. He is a powerful magician, and through his magic he knows I have returned. He is searching for me even now, and he may use his powers to defeat you, Baka, even if the woman who directed him has been arrested. We must not alert that man, for then we may not ever find him out. And lastly, I do not think the woman whom I saw was merely paying an assassin. Perhaps that was part of it, but there was something more. Remember that the woman also gave the man a package. If she were doing nothing more than paying an assassin, what was in the package? The murder weapon? I think it quite unlikely."

"Maybe the package contained evidence," Jon said. "Maybe they want to frame somebody for trying to murder Baka, and they're going to plant fake evidence in somebody's house, so they can prove he's guilty."

"Very good," said Neb. "That is exactly what I was thinking. Unfortunately, though, I don't think we have any way to guess what type of evidence it is. It could be almost anything."

Baka looked skeptical and seemed about to reply, but Jon couldn't wait any longer to tell what he had found out.

"Hey, wait till you hear what I just saw!" he said.

Jon told Neb and Baka about the secret tunnel to the women's quarters and about the woman whom he had seen there. From Jon's description of the woman and the location of her chamber, Neb identified her as Khufu's wife Senna, the mother of the king's half-brother Khaf-Ra.

"Are you sure?" asked Baka.

"Yes," said Neb. "I am."

Baka thought a moment. "Alright," he said. "Senna has a motive, but so does Hetep, and my intuition still says Hetep is the guilty one. Besides, Neb, as you would say, we don't know how to interpret what Jon saw. He saw a man come out of Lady Senna's chamber. Who was the man? Was he an assassin? Not necessarily. He could have been her lover, for all we know."

"But she's the queen whose spirit attacked me at the museum," Jon said. "That's no coincidence. I know she's up to something bad."

Jon wasted no time in returning to the women's quarters. As before, he posted himself behind the statue in the corner down the corridor from Senna's chamber door. She was in her chamber now, but earlier he had overheard her talking to her slaves, and he knew she would be going out eventually to meet someone. Jon decided to wait as long as it would take. Even if Senna was not the one responsible for the attacks on Baka, Jon knew she must have had some reason for trying to prevent him from reaching the sphinx at the museum. He needed to expose her plans. He knew he had to search her room, and it would have to be today.

A long time passed — at least an hour, maybe two; Jon wasn't sure. Senna's door opened, and Senna emerged, accompanied by three female slaves. Jon watched as they disappeared down the corridor.

When Jon was sure that Senna wasn't returning to her room, he quickly ran to her door and opened it. The room was magnificent, and very large. Closing the door behind him, Jon slowly approached the oversized bed, which was big enough for at least four people to lie comfortably with room to spare. At either side of the bed there was a stand containing a large fan with a long handle. Jon imagined slaves holding the two fans and fanning the queen as she reclined in her bed.

He looked around the room. The walls were painted with colorful scenes of men and women, kings and queens, gods and goddesses. There were several richly-decorated chairs, and several low tables. One table had a gaming board that looked like backgammon and another board with playing pieces in the shapes of animals.

In one corner there was a bowl of burning incense, which filled the room with its sweet fragrance. Next to the incense bowl there was a table with nine small statues of gods and goddesses. There was a statue of falcon-headed Horus, of jackal-headed Anubis, and of Sekhmet with her lioness's head. There was one of a woman with cow's horns and another of a man with arms crossed like a mummy. There were a cat, a frog, a crocodile, and a ram.

A dressing table stood along one wall of the room, and on the table was a mirror made of shiny metal. Near the mirror was a golden headdress. On the front of the headdress was the image of a bird with a long, curved neck. Jon recognized the bird as a vulture.

On the dressing table was an assortment of jars containing makeup of various colors: red, green, blue, and black. There were perfumes, creams, and ointments. And there was jewelry. Jon examined each item. Nothing seemed unusual.

One table had writing utensils: reed pens, ink, and papyrus on which to write. There were two letters, and Jon read them both. Their contents were not unusual in any way.

He searched through Senna's wardrobe. He searched behind the furniture. He looked at the undersides of the richly ornamented chairs. He went over to the table next to the burning incense. He picked up each of the nine statues on the tabletop and examined each one closely. Each was beautiful in its own way. Something drew him to the statues, something deep within his heart telling him that the statues were the key to finding what he sought. He picked up every statue once again but still found nothing. He was just about to give up when he noticed that the Anubis statue felt lighter than the rest.

He held the statue of Anubis in his hand, examining it more closely. It was made of some metal overlaid with gold, and it had a pair of bright blue jewels for eyes. He lifted the statue in his hand. It definitely felt too light for its size.

He tapped the bottom of the statue on the tabletop. It made a hollow sound. He turned the statue over and over in his hand. There it was! On the underside of the statue there was a fine crack, just barely visible. He noticed four pins on the dressing table nearby. He took one and tried to insert it into the crack in the Anubis statue.

Just then, Jon heard a noise in the corridor outside Senna's door. There were footsteps coming. He knew he didn't have much time. Hastily he tried to pry the statue open with the pin.

The pin dropped. He glanced at the floor but couldn't find the fallen pin. He strained to listen to the noises outside the door. Two women were talking. One laughed.

There was silence. And then, a soft knock at the door.

Jon held his breath.

Another knock. And silence once again.

Jon knew he couldn't stay in Senna's room much longer, but he couldn't give up now. He returned to the dressing table and took another pin.

He struggled to insert the pin into the crack at the base of the Anubis statue, but his palms were sweaty, and his hands were shaking. He steadied himself and wiped his hands on his linen garment. He tried again to insert the pin into the crack, but the pin slipped and stuck him.

The sounds outside the door again caught Jon's attention. He listened. There were two pairs of footsteps. They were leaving.

Jon put his bleeding finger to his mouth and licked the blood away. A thought occurred to him: why was his finger bleeding at all? Shouldn't Neb's magic have protected him from harm? He remembered Neb saying that the magic spell would not protect from accidental injury, but only from attack and injury by a weapon or a living enemy. Before, while running from the guards, he had injured his knee. That was an accident; but wasn't a pin a kind of weapon? Or was it? Anyway, there wasn't time to think about it now, and Jon again turned his attention to the Anubis statue in his hand. He turned the statue over and gently ran the pin along the crack. He found one spot where the crack was slightly wider, and now he was able to insert the pin. The statue opened, and a small jar fell out.

The jar resembled some of the perfume bottles on the dressing table, except that it was tightly sealed, and the image of a vulture was engraved on the front of the jar. Quickly he closed the base of the Anubis statue and put the statue in its place. He kept the jar.

He opened the door a crack. There was nobody in sight. He opened the door and stepped into the corridor.

He was about to close the door when he heard a sound, the sound of someone lurking just behind the open door. Instinctively he spun around and saw a woman lunging at him, a dagger in her hand. Jon tried to jump aside, but he lost his balance and fell forward at the woman's feet. She tried to stab at him again, but he seized her ankle and rolled away. The woman fell down, the dagger clattering to the floor out of her reach.

Jon took the dagger and quickly rose. The woman also began to rise. She turned her face toward Jon. Their eyes met momentarily, and both recognized each other.

"What are you doing here?" the woman said, apparently surprised to see him.

But Jon didn't answer. He turned and ran. After he had rounded the corner and was half-way down the next corridor, he looked back to see if anyone was following. Surprisingly, nobody was there. Still, he wasn't taking any chances; he continued running till he reached the secret tunnel entrance.

Jon burst into Baka's secret room and shut the door. "I think I have the evidence we need. And now I know who the woman is."

"What do you mean, Jonathan?" Neb asked, but something in Neb's tone of voice told Jon that Neb already knew.

"I told you, Neb: I found the woman who was trying to kill Baka. It's the same woman I saw earlier today, the same queen who tried to stop me in the museum. You said her name is Senna. I sneaked into her room and looked around. She caught me just as I was leaving and tried to stab me. Don't worry; she didn't get me. I guess she would have, though, but luckily I fell, and that's why her dagger missed."

Neb's ear twitched, and Jon noticed the faint suggestion of a smile at the corner of the sphinx's lips.

"Hey, wait a minute!" Jon exclaimed. "I was wondering why I suddenly lost my balance then. That wasn't luck at all, was it? That was you protecting me!"

Neb said nothing. He didn't even nod. But Jon now saw a twinkle in the sphinx's eye, and that was enough for him. He had his answer.

"Anyway, here's the evidence I found in Senna's room," Jon said. "I don't know what it is exactly, but it looked suspicious." He stretched out his hand to Neb. Lying in his palm was the jar he had taken from Senna's chamber.

Neb looked at the jar and at the vulture image that was engraved upon it. "It is the goddess Mut," he said, almost in a whisper. And Jon noticed how Neb's face suddenly turned pale.

"Who's that?" Jon asked.

Neb looked at Jon. "Why, Mut is the vulture-headed goddess, the mother of all Egypt, the mother of the king. But Mut is more than that; she is a paradox. Sometimes she has a vulture's head, sometimes a lioness's. As a vulture, the queens of Egypt wear her form upon their crowns. As mother of the king, Mut gives us life. She gives the land of Egypt life. And yet, her symbol is the vulture, the bird of Death. I think I know what's in the jar."

Neb paused, but neither Jon nor Baka spoke. They both watched Neb, waiting for his next words.

The sphinx continued: "I see the jar is sealed. Be careful, Jonathan. Unseal the jar, but do not let the liquid spill, and do not let it touch your skin."

Jon did as he was told. When he had the jar open, Jon brought it closer to Neb.

Neb smelled the odor coming from the jar. For a moment, Neb said nothing. Then, in a soft and shaking voice, he said, "Quickly, close the jar."

"What is it, Neb?" Jon asked as he sealed the jar again.

"It is just as I suspected. It is the poison that was used to murder me. It is the poison known as *metut An!*"

CHAPTER 18

THE LETTER

The same day, shortly after

The scribe Ahmose sat in Senna's chamber. His legs were crossed, and a writing board was on his lap, a sheet of papyrus spread out upon the board ready for Ahmose to fill with written words. His face was calm, expressionless, betraying not the slightest hint of the haste with which he had been brought to Senna's chamber. Patiently he watched Senna and waited for her to begin dictating the letter. She was pacing back and forth, deep in thought. The late afternoon sun shone through Senna's window and bathed her face in light. A tear formed at the corner of her eye and began to trickle down her cheek. She didn't wipe the tear away.

Senna stopped pacing and looked at the scribe. She began to speak. Ahmose wrote her words:

My love,

I fear I am discovered, and my life is in great danger. When I returned to my chamber this afternoon, I discovered an intruder just as he was leaving. I stabbed at him with my dagger, but he was too swift for me. He threw me to the floor, and I saw his face: it was Prince Baka. Now I dared not scream and call the guards, for I thought it likely that the guards would take me into custody rather than the prince. I was powerless to stop him from escaping.

I entered my chamber, and immediately I noticed a pin lying on the floor far from the dressing table where it should have been. I ran to the place where I had hidden the jar of Mut's elixir. The jar was gone.

I know that it will not take long for Baka to discover what the jar contains, and then I fear the guards will come for me at any moment. Do not try to save me; you cannot. If you try, you will only put yourself in danger, and that you must not do. No matter what my fate may be, you must not allow our plan to fail. You will do your duty, as I will do mine.

Live on, my love. And if I die, promise me that you will finish what we have begun. Swear that you will carry out our plan when I am gone. Then my death will not have been in vain.

Ahmose packed up his ink, his reed pen, and his writing tablet. When the ink had dried on the papyrus, he rolled it up and bound it.

Ahmose had been a royal scribe since Senna's childhood. He had watched her growing up. She had always been a strong-willed person. Even as a child, she had never wavered, never faltered, never cried.

Senna put one hand on each of Ahmose's shoulders. Her grip was firm. "Look at me, Ahmose. I want you to remember me as I am today."

Ahmose looked up. He looked at Senna's face. She was crying.

"Give the letter to him yourself. Make sure you are not seen. At sunset he will be at the Temple of Ptah, in the place where the god hears prayers. Go down the steps, to the second of the private prayer rooms. Wait until the man comes out. You know the signals that you must use. When he has read the letter, make him swear an oath to you that he will do as I have asked. Do not try to see his face or find out who he is. Return to me immediately. Speak to no one else. I shall await your coming."

Of all the temples in Memphis, that of Ptah, the creator god, was the biggest and most magnificent. Ahmose had often admired the beauty of the temple garden with its well-kept paths and trees of every kind. But today he paid no attention to the garden's beauty. He took the straightest path through the temple garden and entered the great stone building between its many massive columns, into the hall within. In the distance, from within the temple sanctuary, he heard the melodious chanting of the priests preparing for their evening offering to the god. He turned away from the chanting voices and quickly descended the steps near the northern wall.

At the foot of the steps, Ahmose found himself in a corridor adjoining several prayer rooms. The only light that reached the corridor was the waning sunlight coming from the staircase.

Ahmose waited in the semi-darkness. It was several minutes before a man emerged from the second room. In the dim light Ahmose could not distinguish the man's features.

"I come from Mut the vulture-headed," Ahmose whispered.

"Anubis hears," said the man.

Ahmose gave the man Senna's letter. "When you have read this, return to me," he said. "I must speak with you."

The man took the letter and nodded. Ahmose entered the private prayer room, while the man climbed the stairs, to read the letter in the light. Ahmose said a prayer and then waited another minute before leaving the room. When Ahmose again emerged into the corridor, the man was waiting for him.

"I will not let her die a shameful death," said the man. "I must go to save her."

"You read her letter. There is nothing you can do. Now swear to me, as she commanded you to do."

"What oath shall I swear?"

"Swear by Ptah, and Set, and Mut. Swear that you will not do anything to try to save the lady. Swear that you will carry out her plan, no matter what."

The man did not answer immediately. Instead, he paced the corridor, opening and closing his fist several times. When finally he answered, his voice was strained. "Alright then, as I love her I will swear by Ptah, and Set, and Mut. I swear that I will do as she commanded. She will not die in vain."

Ahmose returned to Senna's chamber and repeated to her the oath that the man had sworn. Senna nodded her head.

The scribe left Senna's room, knowing he would never see her alive again. Senna was a proud woman, and Ahmose knew she would not want to face a shameful death. She had not told the scribe the nature of her crime, but he thought he could well guess. Slowly, sadly he walked away from Senna's room, knowing what she was about to do. For in the corner of her chamber, Ahmose had seen a cage, and in the cage a deadly snake, waiting to send Senna on her journey to the Western Lands.

CHAPTER 19

ESCAPE

Prince Hur's house, later that evening

P rince Hur looked up from the game board. He had been trying to relax, playing a game against himself, when a loud knock at the door broke his concentration. After Sobek's interrogation that morning, anything out of the ordinary would have been enough to startle him.

"Enter," he said, trying to keep his fear from showing in his voice.

A slave burst into the room and bowed hastily. "Your Lordship, please pardon me, interrupting you like this. I know the hour's late, and you're busy and all, but I thought you'd best know right away. There's been some terrible news, my Lord."

Hur rose from his seat. "Out with it, man! What's the news?"

The slave was trembling. "It's Lady Senna. She's dead."

Prince Hur lowered himself into his seat again. His face was pale. "How?" he asked, his voice a mere whisper.

"Killed by a snake, they say. Sobek's investigating. That was no accident either, Sobek says. It was murder or suicide, so he says."

"When did it happen?"

The slave looked somewhat embarrassed. "They say it was round about nightfall, My Lord. But they were trying to keep it secret, so it took an hour or two before I found out. I came as fast as I could. Anyway, it's still supposed to be a secret even now, but I've got my ways of finding out these things, as you know, Sir."

Hur drummed his fingers on the table. "Yes, this does change things," he said.

"Wait, My Lord, there's more to tell. You've only just heard the half of it. Can I go on?"

Hur nodded.

"There's been another murder, too," said the slave.

Hur sat up straight. "Who? And when?" He was nearly shouting.

"Well, I didn't think much of it at first," said the slave. "It was earlier today. And the victim was an unknown man, found dead in the desert just outside of Memphis. Got his throat slit. Anyway, it didn't mean a thing to me till I heard that bit about the Lady Senna. Two murders in one day! That's not just chance, no it isn't. There's some connection there, I tell you, Sir. Can't say what it is yet; but by the gods, I say there's some connection between those deaths."

Hur leaned forward. "Is anything known about the murdered man?"

"As I told you, Sir, nobody knows who he was. Not a high-class type, though. I can tell you that. By what they say, it sounds to me that he was one of those folks that hang around the piers at night. Not the sort you'd want to meet in some dark alley. Probably got into a goodly many fights and all. He looked that type, they say. He had a crooked nose, kind of bashed in. Oh, and one more thing: he's got a big scar running down his face, like this." The slave swept his finger across his own face, from his left ear down to the corner of his mouth.

Hur thought about that last piece of information. He didn't think he knew the man, but he didn't think it mattered much. Either way, the situation was very dangerous for him, and he knew it would not be long before Sobek paid him a visit again. And, in spite of all Hur's wisdom and his knowledge of the magic arts, if Sobek were to arrest him and charge him with a crime, Hur knew that nothing would be able to save him from his doom.

Hur got up and paced the floor. The slave waited silently, kneeling.

Hur stopped pacing. "Wake the household," he commanded. "Then go to the river and prepare my ship. Make sure you are not seen. We leave before the dawn. Now quickly, go!"

The next few hours were spent in hasty preparation: packing boxes for the journey and loading them into a donkey cart outside, giving instructions to the two or three most trusted slaves who would manage his household while he was gone, and writing letters to be sent to several of his closest friends so that his business affairs would be kept in order in his absence. Finally, two hours before dawn, everything was ready.

A sedan chair waited at the back door of Hur's house. The chair had room for two people to sit. A pair of long poles was attached to the underside of the chair, and brawny, shaven-headed slaves stood at the two ends of each pole, waiting to provide their master transportation. Hur and his wife sat down in the chair. The four slaves hoisted the poles in the air and placed them on their bare shoulders with such ease that it almost seemed they were carrying no weight at all. The slave who had informed Hur of Senna's death drove the donkey cart some distance behind the sedan chair. A pair of female slaves walked behind the cart. A lone male slave walked in front of the sedan chair, his hands free, a long dagger hanging at his side.

Silently they walked along the dark streets of Memphis, never talking, watching every house and every alley for any unexpected motion. Hur felt the tension of the slaves, just as they felt his. He felt the evil forces of the night, blowing past him on the hot desert wind. He felt his wife's arm around his waist. He knew that she was also frightened, and yet her arm around him soothed his tension. But only for a moment.

Somebody or something moved suddenly along one of the side streets as they approached. The slaves saw it too. They put down the sedan chair and stood with tightened muscles, ready for a fight.

The slave in front had his dagger drawn. He moved slowly towards the side street, looking left and right. There was nothing. Soon the slaves hoisted the sedan chair up again, resuming their journey. Perhaps the motion along the side street was just a cat. But Hur did not think so.

They didn't dare take a direct route to the river. Hur thought it best to zigzag through the streets, just in case they were being watched. It took almost an hour to reach the river's edge.

As they approached the pier, a man came into view. Hur's slaves stopped abruptly, watching. The man was singing loudly to himself. He swayed as he walked. Obviously a drunken sailor.

Hur's slaves waited for the sailor to pass before moving forward again. Cautiously they approached the pier.

Hur's ship was easily the largest vessel docked in that part of the river. It was a beautiful ship, with its tall mast and spacious deck;

and Hur was very proud of it. He had spent many pleasant days on board, sometimes on business trips, sometimes on pleasure cruises up and down the Nile. His heart throbbed when he saw the majestic ship which was almost a second home to him. It was all equipped and was waiting for its master. Soon everything would be alright. He would be under way, sailing up the Nile river, south toward Thebes where he would be safe.

The slaves put the sedan chair down. Hur wanted to run to the ship, but he contained himself. His wife stepped out of the chair, and he took her hand in his. They walked along the pier to the waiting ship. The slaves followed.

Hur sensed something move behind him. He spun around to face the motion. Six men were advancing towards him with drawn swords.

The male slaves ran to protect their master. Hur quickly turned from the six men, grasped his wife's hand more tightly, and walked rapidly to his ship. He thought he could make it before the armed men caught up with him.

In front of him and slightly to his left, suddenly he heard another sound, the sound of a sword being drawn from its scabbard. Hur turned towards the sound.

The man who had drawn the sword was standing in the shadows. Six more men stood behind him. The man was smiling, and Hur could see his teeth gleaming in the moonlight.

"Going somewhere, Your Highness?" said the man as he moved out of the shadow.

Hur recognized the voice before he saw the face. It was Sobek, Captain of the Palace Guard.

The six men behind Sobek fanned out, blocking Hur's path to the ship. The six men behind Hur also fanned out, blocking his retreat.

Sobek pointed his sword directly at the prince and said: "Hur, son of Khufu, I arrest you in the name of King Djedef-Ra, Lord of the Two Lands; I hereby charge you with the attempted murder of Crown Prince Baka, and with the murder of Neb the king's vizier."

CHAPTER 20

THE TRIAL

One day later

The Great Hall was filled with people. Some were conversing with each other, but most sat silently, their eyes fixed on the platform at the front of the hall. Slowly, solemnly, King Djedef-Ra entered from behind the platform and took his seat on his throne. Queen Tenka, the King's Principal Wife, entered from the opposite side and took her seat to the king's left.

At the foot of the platform's three steps, the Magistrate of the Royal Court stood at one side, while a royal scribe stood at the opposite side. The magistrate held a staff in his right hand. The scribe held a papyrus roll in his.

The center of the hall was vacant, and the audience sat at either side, facing the center. Jon, dressed in Baka's garments, sat in the first row. Neb, invisible, watched from the far corner of the hall.

A trumpet sounded, and the prisoner was led in by a pair of armored guards. The prisoner was brought to the middle of the Great Hall, where he was made to stand facing the king.

At a nod from the king, the magistrate and the royal scribe came forward. Slowly, rhythmically, the magistrate thumped his staff on the floor three times, and the sound resonated through the hall. The magistrate shifted his staff to his other hand.

"The royal Court is now in session," he announced. "By authority of the son of Ra, King Djedef-Ra Lord of the Two Lands, the royal scribe will read the charges."

The scribe unrolled his papyrus document and read aloud: "Hur, son of Khufu, brother of King Djedef-Ra, you stand accused of the murder of Neb, the king's vizier."

"How do you plead?" the magistrate intoned.

Hur looked at the king and answered, "Not guilty."

The scribe continued: "You also stand accused of plotting the murder of Crown Prince Baka, Son of the King's Body, and on two occasions attempting to carry out that murder."

The magistrate thumped his staff on the floor again and said, "In this matter, Hur son of Khufu, how do you plead?"

"Not guilty."

Normally the case would have been tried before a panel of judges, but this was no ordinary trial. Because of the high position of the defendant, and because of the sensitive nature of the accusations, the king himself was to be the sole judge.

King Djedf-Ra sat on his throne. In his right hand he held a curved rod, a shepherd's crook; in his left hand, he held the *ankh*, symbol of life. He looked at his half-brother and spoke:

"Ever since our father Khufu died, several of my brothers have opposed my kingship. Whether because of jealousy or greed, whether for the love of power or the hatred of your king, in the past you were among the leaders in the fight to overthrow me. Hur, my brother, you are known for wisdom. And you are known for mastery of the magic arts. You, who were vizier in the final days of our father's reign, should have known better than to abuse your power and your wisdom.

"I spared your life then, eight years ago. I thought that you had learned your lesson and that your wisdom would prevail. But here you are again, standing before me in this court, once more accused of plotting against your king. I ask you, Hur: what am I to think?"

"It is a lie, my brother."

"We shall see," said the king. "I make no judgement yet."

The king turned to his right and nodded. "Captain of the Palace Guard," he said, "Present the evidence."

Sobek came forward. In his hands he held three packages wrapped in papyrus. He put the packages down on a small table. He bowed to the king and then carefully unwrapped the first package but left the wrapping still loosely covering the contents.

Sobek recounted the events of the last few days, including his interrogation of Prince Hur at the palace and his request that Hur produce records documenting his activities at the time of Neb's murder. He told of Hur's attempted escape and of his arrest.

Sobek now paused and looked around the hall, his eyes making contact with the audience. Then he turned to the king and said, "Your Majesty, when Neb's body was discovered, there were two puzzling findings that were not publicly revealed until today. The first one was the absence of Neb's signet ring. Besides its use for signing official documents, Neb's ring was said to possess magic powers. All of Egypt knew of Neb's great magic, but only very few knew about the power of his ring. Neb always wore it, but when his body was discovered, it was missing from his hand. Yesterday, after I arrested Hur, I went to his home with a royal scribe. I searched the house, and the scribe recorded what I found."

With a rapid motion, Sobek pulled away the papyrus covering the contents of the first package. He took the exposed object in his hand and held it up for all to see.

"This is Neb's ring. I found it hidden in a secret compartment within the doorpost of Prince Hur's house."

The audience began to murmur, and the magistrate had to pound with his staff many times before silence was restored.

As though there had been no interruption, Sobek continued: "The second puzzling finding at Neb's murder site was the presence of incense. On close examination of the vizier's body, I discovered a few grains of incense adhering to his robes. It was a special sort of incense, an extremely rare variety, and I recognized it by its peculiar odor as an incense used by priests in the worship of Anubis. Shortly after Neb's assassination, we searched Neb's home but found no implements or incense of Anubis's cult. I therefore thought it likely that the grains of incense on Neb's garment had come from his assassin. I looked for the assassin among the priests in the temple of Anubis, but I looked in vain It was not until this week, in searching Prince Hur's house, that I found the evidence I needed to make the pieces of the puzzle fit together. Two days ago, while I interrogated Prince Hur, unbeknownst to him my soldiers searched his house."

Sobek removed the papyrus cover from the second object on the table and revealed a jackal mask. Again, murmurs were audible among the audience, but Sobek ignored them.

"By itself, this Anubis mask proves nothing," Sobek said. "But the mask raised questions in my mind and made me wonder what

I might find if I would search the prince's home more thoroughly. It turns out that I got my answer on the following day."

Sobek paused to unwrap the third package. His eyes scanned the hall as he extracted the object within and held it closed tightly in his fist.

"Your Majesty, in searching Hur's home yesterday after his arrest, in addition to Neb's signet ring which I have already shown you, I found a second object hidden in the crevice in the doorpost."

Sobek held the object high for all to see. "It is a jar of incense, Your Majesty. It is the same incense that was found adhering to Neb's robes on the day we found him murdered."

Again the magistrate had to bang on the floor with his staff repeatedly to call the court to order. When all were silent, the king asked:

"Please tell the court, Captain, what role you think this incense played in the murder of the king's vizier."

Sobek waved his hand in a sweeping motion. "In fact, Your Majesty, the presence of this jar of incense hidden in Hur's house would cast suspicion on the prince even if we were unable to explain the role that incense might have played in Neb's assassination. However, as it happens, I do have a theory.

"As mentioned, this type of incense is extremely rare. It is used only in the worship of Anubis. Prince Hur had a special love for the jackal-headed god, and often he went to the temple of Anubis. It is my opinion that Hur employed the incense to invoke the power of the god to overcome his enemy the vizier."

"And what, in your opinion, was Hur's motive for the murder?" asked the king.

"It is my contention that Hur was plotting to overthrow the king. But there was one obstacle standing in his way, and that obstacle was Neb. Hur knew that Neb's magic powers would protect the king, and therefore he needed to eliminate Neb first. But in addition, since Hur himself had been vizier until Your Majesty dismissed him from that post, I think Hur had great pleasure taking his revenge upon the man who had replaced him."

The king said, "Captain, so far all your evidence has been indirect, circumstantial. The signet ring, the mask, the jar of incense, and the prince's previous actions certainly are suggestive and suspicious. And yet, the evidence is not sufficient to convict the prince. Captain, has your investigation yielded any proof of a more direct nature?"

Sobek smiled a toothy smile. "Indeed it has, Your Majesty," he said.

Several witnesses were then brought into court. The first one, an employee in Hur's household, testified that he had seen Hur meeting with a large man the day before the crown prince was attacked in bed. The witness said that Hur had paid the man some money, but the witness had thought nothing of the matter until yesterday when Sobek questioned him and showed him a sketch of the attacker. The attacker was the same person Hur had paid the night before, the witness said.

The second witness was a man unknown to Hur, a man who said he happened to be present at an inn where Hur was meeting with some friends, the day before Neb's death. After Hur had drunk a fair amount of beer, the second witness said, there was some talk about the king.

Sobek approached the witness standing in the witness box and said softly, "Can you tell this court exactly what was said about the king?"

"Well," said the witness, "I can't say I remember everything that was said. But there's one thing I remember well."

"And what is that?" Sobek asked.

The witness hesitated for a moment. He glanced at the king. Then he looked at Sobek again. His voice trembled as he said, "One of the men sitting at the prince's table said that many in the royal family still opposed King Djedef-Ra, and it was only thanks to Neb's protection that the king still had his throne."

"Can you identify the man who spoke those words?"

"No, I can't. I didn't get a good look at him."

"And did Prince Hur give any answer when those words were spoken?" Sobek asked.

"Yes," the witness answered. His voice was steady now. "The prince said, 'Don't worry. Anubis will take care of everything.'"

"Why did you not report this conversation to the authorities?" the king interrupted..

The witness seemed a bit shaken by the king's question, but he quickly recovered his composure and answered, "It seemed like just a lot of harmless talk, Your Majesty. Just discussing politics, I thought. And as for that last bit about Anubis, I couldn't figure that one out at all. But there's never any harm in saying the gods will take care of things, is there?"

The third, and last, witness was most damaging to Hur. He was a merchant who said he had been traveling through the desert on the day of Neb's assassination when he had come across some men standing next to a statue. Being naturally curious, the merchant said he had moved closer, being careful not to be seen.

"What kind of statue was it?" asked the king.

"It had a man's face and a lion's body. It's one of those new types of statues; a sphinx is what I think they call it."

"Did you recognize the sphinx's face?" asked the king.

"Oh, sure. He's famous; everybody knows his face. Neb, Your Majesty's vizier that was. I'd know him anywhere."

"Did you recognize any of the men?"

The merchant pointed at the prisoner. "Recognized one of them at least. Prince Hur it was. He's famous too."

"And what were the men saying? Were you able to hear them?"

"Couldn't hear the whole of it, Your Majesty, but I did hear some. Prince Hur was asking if all was ready; and 'When will the *Tjaty* be arriving?' he asks."

"Was that all?"

"Just about. Then one of the other men gives Prince Hur a mask, and they all go down into a stone doorway. They just disappeared through that door. I guess it led to some underground crypt or temple. I didn't get any closer to see. Too risky, I figured, and so I just got out of there."

"One last question," said the king. "Did you see what kind of mask it was?"

"Yeah. I mean I did, Your Majesty. It was an Anubis mask."

At this testimony, the crowd's emotions burst into heated conversation. The magistrate pounded on the floor with his staff again and again, to no avail. Even Hur, who had stood silently until now, waiting for his turn to speak, now could hold himself no longer.

"It is a lie!" Hur shouted. "They are all lies!"

When order was finally restored, the king called Hur to testify on his own behalf. Hur swore that he was innocent of both charges. He swore that he had never met the man who had attacked the crown prince in his bed. He swore he had not cast a spell on Neb or confronted the vizier wearing a jackal mask. Hur brought witnesses verifying his faithfulness to the king. But in the end, Sobek's evidence proved overwhelming. Hur was convicted and sentenced to die by the sword in one week's time.

CHAPTER 21

MAKING PLANS

Baka's hidden room, that evening

"It's not right," said Baka. "I just can't let Jon substitute for me tomorrow." His face seemed strained as he paced the floor of his room. He was now able to walk again, but with some pain and with a noticeable limp.

The sphinx hovered in the air. "I cannot permit you to attend the ceremony. It is too dangerous. But also, no one knows that you were ever injured and that the person who appeared before the people in the last few days was really Jonathan. You must not be seen in public till your injury is completely healed."

Baka stopped pacing. "No. I must!" he said in a firm, commanding voice. "No matter what the danger, I must do my duty. How can I allow anyone to substitute for me when the king officially declares me heir to the throne? How can I allow a substitute when the king proclaims that I am to marry Princess Meres-ankh? Is Jon to marry the princess? Will Jon be king when my father's soul goes to the Western Lands? I am the prince. It is I who will marry Princess Meres-ankh. And it is I who will rule as King of the Two Lands."

"Of course you will," said Neb. "This is not the coronation, and this is not the wedding yet. Tomorrow's ceremony is only a formal announcement of what everybody knows: that the king has chosen his successor. Relax, my prince, and put your mind at ease. Jon will not take your kingdom or your wife. Soon Jon will return to the place from which he came, and you will have your kingdom and your princess and the entire land of Egypt for yourself. But I fear for you tomorrow. The danger is much too great."

Baka became silent. He paced the floor again, throwing glances at the sphinx from time to time. After a long while, Baka again stopped pacing. He glared at the sphinx and turned to Jon.

"Well, Jon, what is your opinion?" he asked.

Jon looked at Baka, puzzled. "I see your point about taking your place at the ceremony, Prince Baka. But I don't understand what both of you are saying about the danger. What are you worried about? Senna's dead, and Hur's in jail, isn't he?"

"That he is," said Baka. "But they have the wrong man."

"What? How can you say that?" Jon asked. "We told you everything that happened at the trial. We told you about the evidence and the witnesses. And Hur has a motive, and a record of plotting against the king. What more do you want?"

"That's the problem. It's just too neat. Somebody is taking advantage of Hur's past record to pin the crime on him, to make us think the enemy has been caught. But the real criminal is still at large. He's counting on us to let our guard down now, and then he'll pounce."

"But what about all the evidence, and the witnesses?"

"The evidence was planted, and the witnesses were bribed. Hur is a very careful man. I don't believe he would leave such evidence in his doorpost, even in a secret compartment."

Neb looked troubled. He twitched his ears. "I share your fears, my prince," he said. "That also was my feeling during the trial, until the last witness testified about the murder scene. He said he saw Hur standing with a jackal mask, outside an underground temple in the desert, awaiting my arrival. That was no false testimony. That is how it really happened."

"Alright, I grant you that," said Baka. "But even so, the witness was false. Remember, Neb, that you are not the only one who knows the truth. There is one other besides you: the murderer. He is the one who bribed the witness and told him what to say."

"That is a possibility," said Neb sadly. "But even if Hur is guilty, I cannot put my mind at ease. Something deep inside me cries a warning, telling me the danger to Prince Baka is not over yet. Hur may be in jail, and Queen Senna may be dead, but there may be an accomplice still at large."

"Be that as it may," said Baka, looking at Neb. "It is still my decision to make. And I choose to attend the ceremony, despite the danger. Jon will not take my place."

Neb rose higher in the air. He arched his back and flicked his tail back and forth. Suddenly a gust of air blew from the sphinx across the room and lifted Baka off the floor. The prince tried to struggle free, but he could not release himself. He was trapped in an invisible cage, hanging in mid-air.

"Let me go!" Baka appeared to be shouting. But the cage of air trapped the prince's voice, and all that was heard outside the cage was a whisper.

Baka kept on struggling for a while, but finally he saw there was no use to that. He sat down, still hanging in mid-air, and glared at Neb. The sphinx continued looking at Baka with a stony expression.

"I hope you are coming to your senses now," said Neb after a few minutes. "I hate to do this to you, my prince, but it is for your own good. I cannot let you attend tomorrow. If you give me your oath to do as I say, I will let you free. But if you will not listen to reason, I will keep you imprisoned in this cage of air until the ceremony is over. The choice is yours, my prince."

Baka stood up again and tried to put his hands on the cage's invisible bars, but he found there were no bars: there was just a solid wall of air. Again he turned his eyes toward the sphinx with a ferocious look. He placed his hands on the invisible wall that surrounded him.

"Alright, you win," he said. "What do you want me to do?"

CHAPTER 22

THE ARROW

The square was filled with many thousands of people. It seemed as though the entire city had turned out to hear the king's announcement. With each passing minute, hundreds more people poured into the square, each trying to position himself for a better view.

At one end of the square was a large stone building with great stone columns. The building opened onto a wide stone stage which was flanked on either side by a pair of towering black stone statues of the lioness-headed goddess Sekhmet. For now, the stage was empty except for a pair of thrones placed in the front center of the stage, looking outward onto the square. The entire square was surrounded by tall columns and by statues of gods and goddesses: falcon-headed Horus and ibis-headed Thoth, cow-headed Hathor and ram-headed Khnum; Osiris, Isis, Ptah, and Set. And at the rear of the great stage was a huge sun-disk made of gold: the image of the sun-god Ra, father and protector of the king.

From the building, trumpets sounded as four trumpeters in bright uniforms stepped out from the between the stone columns that lined the building's entrance. The trumpeters took up positions in front of the columns, two on each side of the entrance, and sounded their trumpets once again. The king's honor guard of soldiers in shining bronze armor marched out of the building in pairs, their spears held high, each pair separating to form two rows of soldiers, one row at either side of the stage. When all the soldiers were in place, the trumpets sounded a long flourish, as Djedef-Ra, son of Ra, Lord of the Two Lands, emerged from between the columns, with Princess Meres-ankh walking at his left, and Jon dressed in Baka's clothing at his right.

The king took his seat at the front of the stage, and the princess sat beside him on his left. Jon stood at the king's right side. Baka, disguised as one of the soldiers in the honor guard, stood behind King Djedef-Ra to his right.

Jon tried to appear as princely as he could. He held his head high and looked out at the crowd, trying not to appear as nervous as he felt. Slowly he turned his head, looking this way and that. Bowmen stood at each corner of the stage, ready to defend the royal family against any attack. Other bowmen stood at several elevated guard posts around the square. The king's bowmen were known far and wide for their speed and skill with bow and arrow, and their presence should have helped to put Jon more at ease. Also, Jon somehow felt the presence of the sphinx, floating invisibly near the stage.

But neither the bowmen nor the sphinx's presence seemed quite enough. Hur was in jail, but Baka had shaken Jon's belief in Hur's guilt. And even if Hur was guilty, who could say how many others were involved? Who could say whether one of the soldiers in the honor guard was right now waiting for his chance to attack?

The trumpets again played a flourish, and King Djedef-Ra raised his hand for silence.

"People of Egypt. This is a joyous day in the Two Lands. For on this day, the future is decided. On this day, the nation's fate is sealed.

"There are men in this kingdom who have risen up against their king and against his chosen son. In their rebellion, these men have sinned against the gods themselves. There is great evil among them, and the powers of darkness follow after them. The leader of the traitors has been caught and will be punished soon. But other traitors still remain, and their evil souls contaminate the land."

The king looked up at the sky as he continued: "I am the son of Ra, and I am Horus here on earth. In my hand I wield the power of Osiris, the power over life and death. I am the mighty one who brings the light of heaven to shine upon the land. I call upon the great god Ra to lay his curse upon the traitors who have sought to bring the Shadow to dwell in the Two Lands."

Djedef-Ra lowered his eyes and looked at the crowd. No one spoke. No one even seemed to breathe. All eyes were on the king. Only the bowmen's eyes darted left and right, ever watchful, scanning the crowd.

Djedef-Ra's lips curled into a smile. "But as I said, my people, today is a joyous day. Today it is my duty and my pleasure to present to you the one whom I have chosen to rule my people when I am gone, after my soul has gone across the river to the Western Lands."

The king stood up, turned toward Jon, and stretched out his hand. As Jon took the king's hand, Djedef-Ra led Jon to the princess. The king stepped back a pace and said, "I, Djedef-Ra, son of Ra, Lord of the Two Lands, declare my son Baka as my co-ruler and my heir. I declare that at the next new moon Prince Baka will be crowned as my successor and will be betrothed to marry Princess Meres-ankh who bears the royal blood."

Jon felt strange and somewhat nervous taking Meres-ankh's hand in his. He imagined himself as prince, imagined himself marrying the princess. But, he also realized, it wasn't something for which he was prepared or which he truly wanted. It was kind of exciting playing the prince for a while, but Jon was glad he wasn't stuck with that job for good.

Prince Baka watched Jon taking Meres-ankh's hand. He wasn't exactly jealous, but somehow it felt strange seeing Jon holding the hand of his future bride. He wished today were over. He wished it were the New Moon already. He wished that he could take his rightful place as co-ruler of Egypt and not have to slink about and hide like a fearful child.

Prince Baka turned his eyes away and looked to the side. Out of the corner of his eye, he saw a bowman nocking an arrow to his bow. For an instant, Baka froze. What did the bowman see? Where was the threat that caused the bowman to draw his bow? Baka's eyes darted across the stage, across the square, but he looked in vain.

Baka again turned his eyes to the side. The bowman raised his arrow, aiming it. Quickly Baka noted the direction of the arrow's aim. Then Prince Baka recognized the bowman: it was Sobek. And all at once, the pieces of the puzzle fit into place in Baka's mind. It was Sobek who had murdered Neb. Sobek was the man with both the power and the opportunity to plant the evidence and to pay the witnesses that convicted Hur. And now his arrow was aimed at Jon. Or was it? By logic, Jon, dressed as Baka, must be Sobek's target, but just as Sobek drew his bow the sun's rays reflected off the golden sun disk behind the king's throne and shone in Sobek's face. Sobek's aim was slightly off: the arrow was aimed at Princess Meres-ankh.

Just then, Jon also looked up. He saw Sobek standing with his bow in hand. Almost before Jon realized what was happening, the arrow was shot from the bow. Jon tried to shout, but no sound came. Quickly he turned, intending to pull himself and Princess Meres-ankh out of the way, but already it was too late. If Baka had not already begun to act before the arrow was released, the princess surely would have been struck down.

As Sobek was drawing his bow, Prince Baka sprang towards Meres-ankh. "No!" he shouted as he leaped into the air with all his strength, paying no attention to the pain in his injured leg. He knocked the princess down as the arrow passed over their heads and buried its point in the chest of one of the guards behind them.

A bowman to the right of the stage heard the shout and quickly turned. As he drew his bow, he saw a guard leap into the air, and he saw the princess being thrown to the floor. Of course, he didn't recognize the prince. He saw the guard begin to rise. There was no time to lose, and the bowman thought he must act quickly, before the crazed guard who had knocked the princess to the floor could do anything more. He had a clear shot now. He had to act! The bowman released his arrow, and the arrow found its mark in Baka's heart.

As Baka fell to the floor, Jon ran to the princess. Meres-ankh, who was halfway on her feet by then, suddenly turned to the right of the stage, pointing, a look of terror on her face. As Jon looked up, he saw Sobek drawing his bow again. Jon wanted to shout, but it was already too late. Sobek released his arrow, and the bowman who had shot the prince fell to ground dead.

Everybody was shouting. Guards were running in all directions. The princess, who had recognized the real Baka by now, was screaming and crying, while the king was trying his best to appear strong as he put his arm around the princess and moved quickly off the stage and into the safety of the building.

Jon dropped to the floor and rolled off the corner of the stage. Above him, he heard a voice. "Quickly, Jonathan, get on my back."

It was the sphinx, still invisible. But Jon didn't need to see the sphinx. He took hold of the sphinx's tail and hauled himself up.

The sphinx rose into the air with Jon on his back. As Jon looked down at the frantic crowd, he saw Sobek smiling. And he also saw something more, something he was sure he could not see if he were not sitting on the sphinx's back. Perhaps the sphinx's power was somehow opening his eyes to see more clearly, for Jon could see a Shadow spreading over the land, spreading outwards in a circle from Sobek's smiling face.

Jon shuddered. He felt the evil in Sobek's smile. He felt the hatred radiating from the Captain's soul. He felt Sobek's magic powers reaching out, probing the air around him, sensing Neb's presence.

Jon now realized, just as Baka had, that Sobek was Neb's murderer. But more than that, Jon knew that Sobek also was the murderer of Baka's brothers, and the marksman who had shot the falcon that attacked Jon in the palace courtyard. And finally, Jon realized it was Sobek who had visited Queen Senna in her chamber and who was her secret lover whose face Jon had not been able to see. Jon knew that Sobek would now do everything in his power to fulfill Queen Senna's plan to kill King Djedef-Ra and place Prince Khaf-Ra, son of Senna and Khufu, upon the throne.

It seemed to Jon that Sobek's victory was now complete. Except for Jon and Baka, no one had seen Sobek shoot the first arrow. The second bowman had shot at Baka not knowing the prince's true identity, and Sobek immediately had turned the situation to his own advantage. Jon knew that Sobek would now claim the other bowman had been among the plotters to kill the prince, while he, Sobek, had acted quickly to protect the princess and had shot the bowman dead. Who would challenge Sobek now? Not Baka: he was dead. Jon wished there were something he could do, but he saw clearly that he was powerless to stop Sobek now. With Baka dead, Jon no longer had any role to play in the palace.

As the sphinx sped away into the desert, Jon's eyes met Sobek's. Sitting on the sphinx's back, Jon knew he was invisible to Sobek, but still he felt Sobek's evil power burning into him, calling to him. Sobek opened his mouth and spread his arms. Jon was sure that no one in the square could hear the words, but far above the ground, the desert air trembled with the sound of Sobek's voice:

"I cannot see you, Neb, but I know that you are here. We are not finished, you and I. I still must test my power against yours, and I will defeat you, *Tjaty*. We will meet again someday."

CHAPTER 23

THE PHOTOGRAPHER

Washington, DC, present time

There was a knock at the hotel-room door, and Jon went to answer it. "Who's there?" he called out as he put his eye to the peep-hole.

"It's Karen," said the voice across the door. "Are you ready yet?"

Karen was one of Congressman Travis's assistants. Jon liked Karen, but he would have preferred to be going with his father or his mother rather than being picked up by his father's assistant.

"There's plenty of time," Jon said as he flung the door wide open.

"Just hurry up anyway," Karen said. "We don't want to be late."

It was two weeks since Jon's return from ancient Egypt, and things were mostly back to normal. He was no longer a prince, and his parents were still ignoring him as always. But he did notice something different about himself since returning from his trip back in time: his attitude was different — more mature, he supposed. Anyway, being ignored by his parents didn't seem to bother him as much as it used to.

The sphinx had brought him back just an eye-blink after he had left. Nobody could have noticed his absence. It was almost as though no time had passed at all, as if his trip to ancient Egypt had never been. But, of course, Jon knew he *had* experienced everything. The memory of his Egyptian adventure was still fresh in his mind two weeks after his return, and the fear and excitement of his escape had not worn off yet, even now. Baka and all the others were long dead, but Jon felt a special bond with Baka, as though the prince were his twin brother. In fact, he felt that something of Baka still lived within him.

Jon finished getting ready and went down to the hotel lobby with Karen. Karen said something to the man at the desk and hurried Jon outside to the hotel driveway, where a car was waiting to take them to the White House. Egypt's new leader, President Hassan, now fully recovered from the assassination attempt of two weeks ago, was visiting Washington, and the president of the United States was to greet the Egyptian president today at a special ceremony on the White House lawn. Congressman Travis was one of the guests at the ceremony, and he had also managed to get passes for his family to attend.

Karen brought Jon to his assigned place. His mother was already there, but she was involved in a discussion with the wife of another congressman, and after giving Jon a quick kiss on the cheek she returned to her conversation.

There were many people on the White House lawn, and Jon recognized only a few of them. But that was fine with him. He enjoyed looking around and observing the crowd.

Nearby there was a group of news reporters and photographers. One of the photographers caught his eye. He was a thin man of medium height, and he was carrying a duffel bag. When another photographer tried to get by, the man with the duffel bag pivoted on one foot and stepped aside to let him pass. Somehow, the extra pivoting motion bothered Jon. He thought the man's way of moving seemed strange: too skittish, too abrupt. In fact, even when standing still, the photographer with the duffel bag appeared to be constantly alert and watchful, his body ready to spring into action. Jon tried to see his face, but the face was turned the other away.

Jon's mother introduced Jon to the son of a senator seated behind her. When Jon turned back again, he saw that the man with the duffel bag was now fidgeting with his camera equipment. A few times, he ran a hand through his thick black hair. He seemed a bit nervous. Maybe he was just impatient for the president to arrive and for the day's events to get started already, but Jon didn't think so. Something about the man made Jon uneasy, and somehow, Jon thought, he looked familiar. If only he would turn around so Jon could see his face!

The man took a memory card out of his shirt pocket and inserted it in his camera. Jon was looking ahead and only occasionally throwing a glance in the photographer's direction, trying not to make his spying on the man too obvious. He figured his suspicions were most likely wrong and that the man was just an ordinary photographer after all. But the uneasy feeling kept on nagging him, nudging at his consciousness.

He looked at the other photographers sitting across the aisle in the press section. They all had their equipment set up, and their cameras were ready to shoot. Suddenly a thought struck Jon: *What kind of photographer would come to an event like this with his camera not yet loaded?*

Jon decided he had to get a better look at this photographer. He moved into the aisle and pretended to trip. The photographer looked in his direction.

Jon couldn't believe his eyes. For a moment, he thought of ducking under a seat, or running away, but he quickly regained his courage and stood his ground. Their eyes met for a moment only, and Jon was surprised that the photographer didn't seem to recognize him. But Jon recognized the photographer. It was a man whose face he would never forget, a man who logically could not be here, who should have died more than four thousand years ago. And yet, his presence here should not have been surprising afer all, for had not Sobek's last words been that they would meet again?

CHAPTER 24

CONFRONTATION

t can't be Sobek, Jon thought. *Sobek would have recognized me.* And yet, something deep inside Jon's heart was telling him that this indeed was Sobek.

Jon thought of his last day in ancient Egypt. He thought of how Sobek had plotted in secret to kill the prince. He thought of Sobek's final threat as he and Neb were making their escape. Sobek must have known that Jon and Neb had come from the future and were escaping back to their own time, and yet Sobek had said they would meet again. Did that mean Sobek had some magic way of transporting himself into the future?

It was almost time for the ceremony to begin. Jon was now back in his seat again, sitting next to his mother. He looked at his wrist watch. In four more minutes, the presidents of the United States and Egypt would arrive and take their places. The photographer held his camera in his left hand. His eyes kept glancing at his duffel bag, which was now slung over his right shoulder. With his right hand he adjusted the strap of the bag. Again, Jon had the impression that something was not right. A real photographer would have put the duffel bag down, to give himself more freedom to move. Maybe he wasn't Sobek, but Jon was sure he was up to something.

Jon tugged at his mother's sleeve and whispered in her ear. "Mom, look at that photographer over there. He's been acting very strange. I think there may be a bomb or something in his bag."

"Come on," his mother said, annoyed. "There goes your imagination again."

"Shh! Not so loud, Mom. He'll hear you. I know him. I've seen him before, and I know he's evil."

But Jon's mother still didn't seem convinced.

Jon looked at his watch again. Three minutes left. He knew he had do something quickly.

Jon got up and ran to his right, into the aisle. This time he didn't trip.

"Hey, Jon. Where are you going?"

"I just have to see something." Jon moved to the other side of the aisle. He leaned over, and his arm brushed against the photographer's duffel bag as he passed.

"Hey, what do you think you're doing? Get your filthy hands off my bag!" the man yelled at Jon, as he grabbed the strap of the duffel bag. He had a foreign accent.

Jon immediately pulled his hand away. "I'm sorry for touching your bag. I didn't mean to."

The photographer stared at Jon a moment but didn't say anything more.

Jon returned to his seat. "See?" he whispered to his mother.

Mom gave Jon an angry look and said, "You had no right to touch that man's bag. Now stay in your seat, and mind your own business."

Two minutes left. Jon pretended to concentrate his attention on the podium where the two presidents would soon appear. But every few seconds he cast a glance in the photographer's direction. The photographer didn't seem to notice him at all.

To the side of the podium, a high school band was filing in, preparing to play when the two presidents arrive.

Jon looked at his watch: one minute left.

The photographer put his bag on the ground next to him.

Now! thought Jon, as he ran quickly into the aisle. He lunged at the duffel bag, grabbed it by the shoulder strap, and started to run with it. The photographer also tried to grab at the shoulder strap but missed. He was very fast, just as Sobek had been, and Jon only barely managed to get away.

Jon started to run towards the back of the aisle, but just then a man got up in the row behind him and stood in the aisle, blocking Jon's path. Jon clutched the bag close to his body and veered around the man.

"Thief!" somebody shouted.

Out of the corner of his eye, Jon spotted a man in a dark suit at the very rear of the long aisle, walking rapidly forward. Jon thought he looked like some kind of undercover agent, perhaps Secret Service. Jon continued running in his direction.

The photographer barreled his way down the aisle, shoving past the man who had blocked Jon's way. The man yelled something, but the photographer ignored him. In seconds, he had just about caught up to Jon. Jon didn't look back, but he felt the photographer's presence close behind, and he tried to dodge.

Again the photographer grabbed at the duffel bag, and this time he succeeded in holding onto the other end of the strap before Jon was able to get clear.

Jon knew he wouldn't be able to get the bag away from the photographer now, but he held on as tightly as he could. The photographer pulled on the bag with his right hand, as his left hand shot out at Jon. Jon jumped out of the way, still holding on to the bag. But, as Jon looked up, he saw Sobek smiling. Sobek, or whoever he was, knew he had won.

"There's a bomb in the bag!" Jon shouted. He pulled on the bag with all his strength.

Sobek still held the bag with his right hand. In his left hand there was a gun. Jon, seeing the gun, let go of the bag and was about to run, but the gun was pointed straight at him. He looked into Sobek's eyes. Sobek smiled viciously.

Jon wished the sphinx were here to help him now. He looked up, and something in Sobek's expression made Jon feel that Sobek knew what he was thinking.

Suddenly, a strong hand slammed down on Sobek's outstretched hand, and the gun fell to the ground with a thud. Sobek turned to his right to face his attacker, but it was too late. The Secret Service man smashed his fist into Sobek's face. Sobek stared at the Secret Service man blankly. His hand began to rise, as if he were about to fight back. Then, without a word, he fell to the floor unconscious.

CHAPTER 25

THE BENU BIRD

Jon was a hero. A bomb was found in the duffel bag, just as Jon had predicted, and the photographer who looked like Sobek — his real name was Abdullah — was arrested.

Abdullah quickly regained consciousness. Handcuffed, he struggled futilely to free himself. He screamed some words that made no sense at all. He seemed crazed, delirious. Two Secret Service men pulled him to his feet. He looked at the arresting officers with wild eyes. He began to chant. The words were not in English, nor in Arabic either, and the tune was exotic, mysterious, haunting. His eyes stared blankly ahead as he again began to scream, this time in English:

"Save me, Senna. The Benu bird must not be released from the grasp of Mut. I have foreseen it, and yet it must not be. The president must die, for I have seen that only when Amir Hassan rules over Egypt will the Benu bird be able to escape his prison."

Of course, everybody thought the terrorist was crazy and his words were meaningless. Even the terrorist himself, when he later came to his senses, claimed not to know the meaning of his own words. But Jon knew otherwise. And he knew those words contained an important clue. He had to tell the sphinx as soon as possible, as soon as he got home from Washington. But that would be tomorrow at the earliest.

That evening, Jon was invited to have a private meeting with the president of the United States and the president of Egypt inside the White House, in the Oval Office. Congressman Travis proudly walked with his hand on Jon's shoulder as he brought his son to meet with the two presidents. When they reached the door to the Oval Office, Jon looked up at his father's beaming face. This was the first time Jon could remember his father showing real pride in anything he had done.

Both presidents shook Jon's hand warmly and thanked him for saving their lives.

The president of the United States said, "That was a very brave thing you did, Jon. Because of you, a dangerous terrorist has been arrested, and the lives of many people have been saved. But it is not only my life and President Hassan's, and the lives of all those people that you have saved. You have also saved the cause of peace in Egypt, and you have saved the world from the rule of terrorism."

Then the president asked Jon how he had known about the bomb, and Jon answered, "It's hard to explain. It's just a feeling that I had, but somehow I was sure of it. I could tell by his face, and the way he was looking at his bag. He seemed really nervous all the time."

When Jon left the White House, a large crowd was waiting. Jon couldn't believe his eyes: there were tens of newspaper reporters, three television crews, and many, many policemen. And they were all waiting for him.

Photographers took his picture. The news reporters gathered around him and asked him questions, all speaking at the same time, so he didn't know whom to answer first. But really, they all had about the same question: "How did you know there was a bomb in the duffel bag?" Jon just smiled at the reporters and mumbled something, but he did not answer their question.

When they got back to their hotel room, Jon's parents continued to ask Jon how he had known about the bomb, but he gave them the same answer he had given the president. He was enjoying all the attention his parents were giving him, and the mystery of how he had known only served to increase their attention further.

Jon and his parents left Washington and returned home the next day, but it was late afternoon by the time they got home, and in the evening some of his father's friends came over to the house. For a change, Jon was the center of attention, and that was a lot of fun. But he was upset because he wasn't able to go to the museum to talk to Neb.

On the following day, Jon returned to school. Between periods and during lunch hour, everybody gathered around him, throwing questions at him from all directions. They were even worse than the newspaper reporters!

One of the girls in Jon's class said, "Come on, Jon. Don't be so mysterious about it. Tell us what really happened. I know it has something to do with that magic sphinx that Mrs. Gunther showed us at the museum. I saw you standing there and looking at that sphinx even when the class moved on. I wondered what you were doing standing there. Now I think I know: it was the sphinx that told you about the photographer with the bomb, wasn't it?"

Jon knew she was just making fun of him, but he answered very seriously: "Yeah, right. It was the sphinx. Do you remember Mrs. Gunther told us the sphinx had a secret? Well, she was right. That's how I knew about the bomb: the sphinx told me his secret."

That night, Jon's parents again were entertaining guests, and Jon could not go to the museum. It was not until the third day after the White House ceremony that Jon finally had the opportunity to sneak out of the house at night. He went to the side of the museum, and again he found the service door open for him. As he made his way among the darkened corridors, he wondered whether Queen Senna's spirit would try to stop him again. He walked slowly, looking in every direction and occasionally glancing behind him, but all was silent. Not a single spirit stalked the halls.

When he reached the sphinx, he thought he saw a smile cross the statue's stony lips.

"Some days ago, I had a vision. I felt the spirit of my enemy approaching. I felt his mind reach out, searching, probing, reaching out to find me. But I stayed silent, hidden from him. He searched in vain. Then, three days ago, again I felt his spirit. I knew he struggled with you. I knew you vanquished him. To my surprise, the magic link that I had spun in Egypt between my soul and yours was not completely gone, and through that link I sensed your victory, your joy, but also something more. I know you have discovered something of importance, a puzzling finding that you feel you need to tell me. But that is all I know. For three days I have waited for you, Jonathan. Even a sphinx can lose his patience."

"I'm sorry, Neb. I couldn't get away. And I'm dying to find out what it all means. I know it must mean something, but I can't figure it out."

Jon quickly told Neb all about the terrorist and about the strange words the terrorist had spoken.

"That's it!" said Neb. "Now I understand everything. And now, I think it will not be long before I find the key to break the spell that holds me prisoner in the sphinx.

"You see, the Benu bird is the bird of resurrection. You probably have heard of him by a different name. The Greeks called that bird the Phoenix and told how every five hundred years he died in fire, only to be born again out of his own ashes.

"The Benu bird is my key to freedom. Do you remember the bottle you found in Senna's room? The bottle was engraved with the image of Mut, and it was Mut's poison that Sobek used to kill me. The spell that Sobek cast upon me was that my soul will be held within the grasp of Mut, imprisoned together with the dying Benu bird so it cannot rise again."

"But what did he mean about President Hassan? What does Hassan have to do with the magic spell?"

Neb smiled again. He twitched his ears. "Ah, Jonathan, the president has everything to do with Sobek's spell, for President Hassan is a descendant of King Djedef-Ra through his daughter, Princess Nefer. Sobek murdered all three sons of Djedef-Ra, but Princess Nefer lived. You see, every spell must have a loophole, a way out. Otherwise, the spell will eventually fall apart by itself. When Sobek cast his spell, he wove a loophole into it, but he clouded my memory so I would forget it. Only now, when you told me the terrorist's words, did I again remember: my soul can be freed from this sphinx only when Djedef-Ra's descendant rules in Egypt."

"But why did he have to attack President Hassan? Couldn't he just attack you directly?"

"That is a very good question, Jonathan. But remember, Sobek couldn't kill me when I was Djedef-Ra's vizier. Now that I am a sphinx, my magic powers have grown immensely, and Sobek knew that a direct attack on me would fail. His only choice, then, was to close the one route to my escape."

The sphinx looked up at Jon. His eyes, though made of stone, looked sad. "And now, Jonathan," he said, "it is time for you to go, and I must give you thanks for all that you have done. From the moment I first saw you, I knew you held the key to my release. You have been very brave. Goodbye, my dear friend."

Jon felt a tear beginning to form in the corner of his eye. He patted the sphinx on the mane and said, "Yeah . . ., bye — for now."

During the next few days, there was no opportunity for Jon to return to the museum again at night, but he did return each day during lunch hour. He stood by the sphinx, hoping to have some sign, but there were many people always bustling about, and Neb did not speak to him. He hoped that was a good sign. Perhaps Neb had left the statue, and the sphinx was just a lifeless piece of stone now. He wished he could know for sure.

For a full week, he wondered about it, and he even dreamt of it at night. Then, one morning, as Jon and his parents were eating breakfast with the radio news in the background, his mother suddenly turned up the volume.

"Hey, listen to this!" she said.

The radio announcer said:

"Sometime last night, burglars entered the Museum of Fine Arts and made off with one of its greatest treasures. The burglary was discovered by a night watchman on patrol at the museum in the early morning hours. There are no clues to the identity of the burglar or burglars. The police and museum authorities are completely puzzled, because there was no sign of any break-in, and it is unclear how the missing item was removed from the museum. But most puzzling of all, only one item was taken. The burglars apparently passed up many smaller objects of great value, objects that would have been much easier to remove. The only missing object is a large limestone sphinx."

THE END

ACKNOWLEDGEMENT

I want to thank my wife Madeline Bavli for her patience and for her invaluable help in editing the manuscript.

Made in the USA
Middletown, DE
12 September 2016